■ RYAN RATLIFF'S

(RELUCTANT) TRIPS THE BOOK SERIES

Published by Aventine Press
55 East Emerson St.
Chula Vista CA 91911
www.aventinepress.com

ISBN: 978-1-59330-853-7

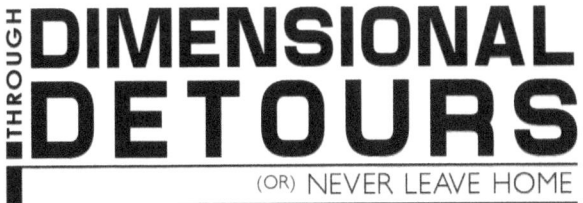

THROUGH DIMENSIONAL DETOURS

(OR) NEVER LEAVE HOME

RYAN RATLIFF

aventine press

**THIS BOOK IS DEDICATED TO
MY LATE FATHER DAVID RATLIFF,
WHO INSPIRED ME TO PURSUE WRITING.**

*And to my mother (Pat), my sister (Vanessa),
my three brothers (Senna, Shane, and Tim),
and my grandfather (Gramps).*

*Thanks to the self-publishing company **Aventine Press**, and Keith Pearson, for helping to publish this book.*

TABLE OF CONTENTS

THE QUARTZ (LIFE'S THE SAME)

■ 3:30PM AUGUST 20TH 1985

On the corner of Seventh and Sunrise not far from the highway can be found The Quartz, a bar that's been in the Chapel family for years; since its inception, in fact, passed down from father to son three times. This time around, Eddie Chapel is the proprietor and has been bartending the small roadside establishment for nearly fifteen years. With his younger brother and fellow bartender, Tim, Eddie has kept The Quartz in Bowling's high favor for just under five years, not long after officially procuring the bar from his late father in nineteen, seventy-eight.

Eddie and Tim have since revamped and modernized The Quartz's image to appeal to the many tourists and temporary locals that blow through the small Arizona town, noting that such a small town wouldn't necessarily require more than one down-trodden old dive, of which it was rife, and instead could use some variation. Among some of their more insightful ideas; hiring flirtatious and attractive waitresses to draw in the crowd. This wasn't before the advent of the cocktail waitress so it couldn't be considered novel in a universal sense, but it was a very new idea to the aging, dust-covered town. Though well-conceived, this idea could never have been perceived as an easy task when considering the relatively low and, at times, considerably unfavorable population of women to be found in Bowling, but the brothers managed, if only through importation.

In addition to the eye appeal of waitresses, the Chapel brothers offer, in terms with the times, some of the most hip décor, inside and out, featuring an interior with walls composed of many uniquely shaped pieces of sheet metal with long flowing wavy designs grinded into the surface. Randomly placed, floating a couple of inches out from the reflective metallic walls are brightly colored fixtures of different basic, two-dimensional shapes like triangles and circles with bright neon lights affixed behind them. The exterior sign displays the bar's name on a similar metal banner with each letter of the name set in a different size and orientation against more brightly colored flat shapes. To accompany these flagrantly trendy features and motif, The Quartz boasts a *mean* sound system to service their *killer* selection of tunes. Above all else, The Quartz prides itself in drink combinations to be found nowhere else, with clever names like *Sheena Easton's Nipple*; 1 ½ oz tequila rose, ½ oz cranberry juice, and ½ oz raspberry liqueur or the *Baracus Beat-em-up*; ½ oz sugar, ½ oz water, 2 ½ oz mango juice, 4 oz pineapple juice, ½ oz dark rum, ½ oz lime juice, ½ oz grenadine, and 2 oz club soda.

On a good night The Quartz will draw around two-hundred customers and around twenty-five hundred dollars. Today is shaping up to be a slow one, even for a Tuesday, but that's alright because Eddie is planning to leave as soon as Tim shows up. He has been promising to take his wife, Jill, to the movies but had been slammed the entire month and knew that if he put it off any longer Jill would make him pay for it in many small, passive-aggressive ways over the next two years. Besides which, he loves her and, for the most part, when not in direct conflict with his own happiness, wants her to be happy.

Tim is late, again. He was supposed to show up at three pm; one hour before happy hour, as was Veronica. Affectionately referred to as Ronnie, the waitress who works the most successful happy hour shifts, Veronica is one of the flirtatious and attractive women the Chapel brothers employed for eye/ buy appeal not long after they procured The Quartz. She also happens to be dating Tim and it goes without saying, whenever

Ronnie is late it generally has something to with Tim. Eddie is upset, but had not planned to see the movie until seven pm, taking into consideration, as always, his brother's general lack of punctuality.

Right at this moment, there are six customers spread about the bar in various places and at various levels of intoxication. Gramps sits down at the far end of the bar and sets down next to him a very old and fairly worn looking transistor radio. This spot is always free until around three-thirty in the afternoon when the old man leaves the quiet solitude of his home for a few hours of semi-social drinking. The stool at the end of the bar has been Gramps reserved seat nearly the entire lifespan of the small drinking establishment. He didn't really care for the new updates to The Quartzsite Bar, as he insists it still be referred, but wasn't quick to make changes to his twenty year routine. Anyways, he likes Eddie and Tim and thought it was about time the bar picked up some business since their father Richard had practically run it into the ground.

"Hey, Gramps, what're ya' having?" Eddie directs to the corner.

"You gotta ask?" Gramps belts out in a gruff and blunt reply.

Eddie pours the twelve year old scotch cleanly over the glass of ice and slides it down to Gramps in a masterfully quick move that reiterates Gramps' belief that Ed is, by far, the best bartender The Quartzsite Bar's ever seen.

"I hate this Goddamn music." Gramps mumbles trailing off as he paws the glass of scotch.

"What's up, Gramps? Somethin' eating you?" Eddie lifts his eye towards Gramps as he hands off two cocktails to another usual.

Gramps replies with a grunt and continues.

"Eh, it's the strangest thing. I went out this morning to look for my old Regency; I was thinking about what Tim had said about his old man's finally giving out, and thought he might like this old radio's been collecting dust in my shed. Soon as I step outside to get it, Pete races to the shed, stops dead in his tracks and starts barkin' like it's the end of the world...Damned dog." Gramps ingests a slow draw from the glass.

"I walk out to him an' nudge him aside a little with my foot an' look in. There's tar all over the damned place."

"Tar? A barrel spill or something?" Eddie leans back against the wall opposite Gramps, wipes his hands on a towel, crosses his arms and stares at the old man's hand as it lazily taps what looks like a dog's collar on the bar.

"No, never even had a drop of tar in that shed. But, anyways, Pete's flipped out an' won't step two feet closer to that shed." Gramps stops to scratch his head and appears to be very deep in concentration trying to recall the event.

"I'll tell you something, if I didn't know any better I'd swear the stuff was movin'. An' it didn't look right neither, I mean it *was* black, but blacker than any tar I've ever seen."

"So..." Gramps sighs briefly before continuing;

"So I go inside the house to grab a bucket of water and a towel, come back out to the shed and the tar's completely gone; wiped clean before I even get there, and so is Pete. Only thing left of him is his collar, or what's left of it." He holds out the tattered collar which now only consists of two short lengths of blue tightly woven bands connected with a tarnished link holding the dog tags.

"I looked everywhere for him, even drove around the block a few times. I don't know...Do you call the police for a missing dog?" Gramps scratches his beard and takes another swig.

"Guess you could call the cops, not likely they'd be able to do anything. You could do like everyone else and post signs— hey, got a picture of Pete? I could post it on the wall right here and let you know if anyone's seen him."

"Yeah...I'll bring one in tomorrow, but I—"

Gramps is interrupted by some apparently unhappy patron.

"Hey, what's the fucking deal here? I've been waiting for the waitress to come around and get my drink."

Eddie thinks to himself; *this prick is already wasted.*

"There is no waitress right now, friend, she's late and I won't be calling anyone else in because, as you can see, it's slow and we don't even have enough customers to fill up the bar." Eddie smirks as he steps closer to the bar; he can smell booze overpowering the guys breath. However, mingling with the dry stench of alcohol is another, even fouler odor Eddie immediately places, with disgust.

"I'm not sittin' at the bar; I'm sitting at the fucking table." The upset bar patron is doing his best to show the bartender he means business, but Eddie is unimpressed, with reason when keeping in mind some of the people who've made a run at him throughout his years behind the bar.

"Honestly, guy, I know it's early, but I think it's about time you head home." Eddie leans in near the inebriated man with focused eyes and peers into the man's face fighting through the fumes of both sources.

"It's barely three o' clock, you kickin' me out? Fuck that." Belligerence seems, to Eddie, to be the man's only mode of operation.

"I'll tell you what, you leave now..." Eddie leans in further and whispers.

"And I won't tell everyone you shit yourself."

"What? What the fu—" The man stops for a second and reaches around touching his wet, warm jeans. He moves his hand across his buttocks and grabs his wallet out of the back pocket. Drawing out a couple of bills he looks wearily at Eddie.

"No thanks man, these are on the house." Eddie smiles and waves his hand over the cash. Gramps can't hold it in and coughs up a loud cackle.

The man dons a petrified look as he returns his cash and wallet. Turning around he mutters "fuck that" once more and edges out through the entrance hoping to go unnoticed.

No such luck.

Instead, he bumps into a tall, large man dressed in flip-flops, shorts and a muscle shirt that reads *Ocean Pacific*.

"Whoa! Buddy, you smell like shit." Michael blurts out as the humiliated man quickly rushes past him through the doorway.

Breaking through an almost uncontrollable bout of laughter Eddie yells, "Hey Mike, what's up, have a seat."

"What the hell was that all about?" Michael plants himself heavily into the seat just beside Gramps.

"Guy shit himself, I guess. Who knows how these things happen?" Eddie chuckles.

"But, hey do me a favor. Wipe up that seat over there."

Eddie retrieves his towel and the soap bucket he keeps under the shelf.

"I'll give you a couple beers."

"Hell, why not, not like it went through his jeans." Michael laughs and grabs the towel and bucket.

"Yeah...better safe than sorry." Eddie, grinning, nods his head towards the seat.

"Eddie, like I was sayin' earlier, I found the transistor radio, kind of scratchy, but it still works great. Tim could make use of it." Gramps picks up his radio and tunes in to the local FM country music station.

"Hey, where is Tim?" Michael sits down and returns to Eddie the towel and bucket.

"God only knows, shouldn't be surprised...He's supposed to cover me tonight."

Eddie wipes the bar with a sort of subconscious movement that only comes with such routinely performed actions and sets down a frosted cold beer on a coaster in front of Michael.

"Ronnie's gone too, huh? 'Nuther big surprise." Michael quickly downs the first beer promised to him; looking to make short work of the offerings.

"Just as long as he shows up before six—hey, speak of the devil." Eddie turns to the door.

Ronnie storms into the building in a fit of rage, throwing the door open.

"Damn it, Tim, you stupid ass...I can't believe you!"

"—like I said earlier, I fucked up the front end of your car and I'll pay for it, but, seriously, it wasn't my fault. I was leaving the bar with Mikey last night and as I was pulling out I saw this cop, and he was shooting at his feet. I turned to Mikey and we both look out his window, he was kind of far away so we couldn't see what the hell he was doing...but it was crazy, I swear he was shooting at his feet." Tim shakes his head and looks at Michael.

Michael nods his head in support and takes another drink.

"Anyways, as I was pulling out, I accidentally hit the light pole. I wasn't watching but—damn, what the hell was that cop doing, he looked like he was going to have a heart attack."

Tim continues his story. "I barely hit it though, and I'll fix the car. You can ask Mikey, that's the God's honest truth."

Tim pleas his case following closely behind Ronnie with his arms out like he's awaiting a hug.

"You were drunk Tim, and I'm sure Mike was too...so excuse me if I don't find the need to have him confirm the same bullshit story. When's your car supposed to be fixed?"

Ronnie leans over the bar and retrieves her apron, stashed in the top shelf behind the bar.

"Ask Mikey, it's at his shop." Tim leans over crossed arms upon the bar next to Mike.

"Oh yeah, about that, they finally got the new clutch, Joe's putting it in today. I told him to call you when it's done." Michael finishes his second freebie.

"Oh, that's right, how *is* your vacation going?" Eddie grabs and trashes the empty bottle.

"Barely started. I'm heading out to the lake tomorrow, probably spend a couple days camping out there—I'll have another one." Michael taps the table.

"This one's on your tab, you'll be wanting to pay that off before you head out, right?" Eddie chuckles and places the bottle on the dampened coaster.

Sitting in the barstool next to Michael, Tim pulls out the contents of his front right pocket which include; several bills, a button, some change, a pocket knife, and a condom.

"I'm covering his tab; he's knocking off fifty for repairing the car." Tim flits out two twenties and a ten to his big brother.

"What the hell is that?!" Ronnie, now wearing her waitress apron, points furiously at the condom sitting on the bar top.

"I'm on the pill, so that sure as hell isn't for me."

"Oh, uh, Mike and I got into some pretty heavy stuff last night." Tim grins hoping Ronnie might be amused by this wisecrack.

"You're such an asshole. Why do you have that condom?" She isn't.

"Why do you always think I'm cheating on you? Some chick at the bar last night was hitting on me, she gave it to me. I shot her down, and that was around the time we headed out. Again, you probably think I'm full of shit, but Mikey was there and neither of us was drunk."

"At which bar were you, anyways? Giving money to our competition?" Eddie rubs his hand into his brother's hair purposely destroying his feathered hair-do.

Tim knocks away his hand. "Yeah I guess we were. There was a band playing at Speedy's Mike wanted to check out. Lame as hell."

Eddie grins, "You know Speedy, man. Guys got no taste in anything except cars"

Michael chuckles "Yeah they were shit, last time I listen to Joe. But don't worry about that chick Ronnie, she was fuckin' heinous. I'd rather pork my hand."

Ronnie rolls her eyes and shakes her head. "So why do you have the condom?"

"What's free is free. I let her buy me a beer too." Tim and Mike both break into laughter almost simultaneously.

"Nice Tim, by the way, you're both about forty minutes late."

Eddie provides the reminder of tardiness in such a manner that it too, conveys great routine.

"Both? Ah shit man, I forgot, no worries, I got you covered. Sorry about that though. We were in Ramsey at the mall, kind of lost track of time—hey, check this out, got a new Walkman." Tim unveils a sleek looking Sony Radio and Cassette Player.

Gramps pipes up "Well I was gonna give you my old Regency...Ah, I guess you might as well have it, that Japanese garbage'll crap out on you sooner'n you know it." Tim stands and walks over to Gramps.

"Hey thanks Gramps, these babies are antiques. The radio on the Walkman's not bad, but I mainly just wanted the tape player."

A pat on the back is applied cordially to Gramps as Tim takes the radio and steps behind the bar. Beneath some towels under the bar counter, Tim buries the two radios as if hiding some valuable treasure.

"You think you can take over now? I'm going to go ahead and take off." Eddie pops open the register and picks up his tickets.

"Yeah, no problem, it's dead as hell anyways—hey, don't worry about that, I'll take care of all that shit. You go ahead and clock out. Tell Jill I said 'Hi'." Tim lights a cigarette and waves his brother off.

"Alright, see you all tomorrow. Don't get into too much trouble at the lake, Mike. Oh and don't forget to bring that picture in Gramps. We'll find Pete for you." Eddie smacks the bar with both hands, walks out from behind it and heads to the door.

Turning back he finalizes his day at the bar; "I'm out! Have fun."

Everybody lets out a short list of pleasantries and good-byes with the only one worth mentioning in detail being Michael's, who says something like; *"Take it easy Eddie, stay off sixth if you can. They got it all blocked off."* Not a typically interesting statement, but it is, nevertheless, prevalent when considering that no road in Bowling has been closed since 1965. And the words become even more relevant when coupled with what Michael proceeds to say after Eddie has departed, having turned around to once again face the bar with Tim now serving the role as his purveyor of poisons.

"Somebody fucked up big time! There's tar all over the road—" Michael stops for a moment pondering the strange quirky smile he's received from Tim before realizing, after a small eternity, the peculiarity in his statement.

"No shit...but seriously, it's like somebody spilt tar all over the road; It's piled up everywhere. But if you ask me it wasn't tar, I don't know, it's one of those things, if you saw it in a picture you wouldn't get it, but seeing it there, right there, something was weird about it, it didn't look right."

"What the hell are you going on ab—?"

Halted mid-sentence, Tim allows by a dazed looking Gramps to interject. His words seem, if only for a moment, to come from a great distance. Tim takes this opportunity to ash his cigarette as he watches Gramps blearily repeat his story.

"There was tar all through my shed this morning. Went to grab something to clean it up with, came back out and it was gone. Now I can't find Pete anywhere."

Gramps had been sitting with an empty glass since he'd been interrupted by the man who could not hold, among other things, his liquor. Needless to say Eddie had tried to fill Gramps glass, much like Tim is now, only to find the same result. Gramps waves his hand dismissively over the glass and returns it to the collar piece. Eddie and Tim both know that the old man's only friend or familiar outside of the bar is his dog, Pete. They also know that Pete would never, for a minute, leave Gramps side. And both know that circumstances in which Pete would be missing would be circumstances that present the unlikelihood of his return. Knowing this, Tim figures he may as well hold off and try serving Gramps again later tonight if he sticks around. But, it's best not to pester a grieving man, even if another glass or two of some fine scotch would create a favorable alternative to his current state.

"I'm real sorry to hear about Pete, Gramps, but like Eddie said, so many people come in and out of The Quartz, we put up a picture and someone's bound to have seen him." Tim makes his efforts to cheer up Gramps.

Michael, against better judgment, or with a possible lacking thereof (as Michael is regularly questioned by others in regards to his ability to possess such judgment) decides to add his two cents.

"Yeah and dogs get lost all the time. I read once, some people lost their dog when they went on vacation, a week later it shows up at their house. Dogs got this thing, you know, they really never get lost, and if they don't come back, it's because they don't want to, or they're—"

"Damn it Mikey, shut the hell up."

Tim looks over at Gramps for a second to ensure he doesn't look too down, is satisfied, and turns to watch Veronica.

He notices, not surprisingly, she seems to have calmed tremendously. Tim had several reasons for breaking the rule of dating an employee. And though, at first, Eddie was reluctant to allow Tim's relationship with an employee of The Quartz; Tim who garnered a vast record of consistent failure in the field of dating and thus could possibly cost them a waitress or two, he knew instantly that Tim was very sincere in his feelings for Veronica. He'd decided that Tim would probably be better off with her than with most of the bimbos to which he would typically devote his attention. Since first meeting Veronica Tim had quickly picked up on what he'd found to be the most appealing traits in a woman, and though anyone who has ever been acquainted with Veronica can relate to most of Tim's sentiments, nobody could ever know just how much they actually mean to him. Tim himself is often completely unaware of exactly how great of an effect Veronica has had on his life, but to most others, it's both clear and appreciated.

As far as Tim's concerned he only needs to know that she's easily the hottest chick in the county, she's easy as hell to talk to, and no self-loving soul could be uncomfortable with her bubbly and inviting personality. And beyond everything else, Tim is the only one who manages to goat her into emotional outbursts and adversely is the only one she's so quick to forgive. In Tim's mind, this latter point implies that she has a genuine love for him, one he shares threefold.

It also works to Tim's favor that Veronica is the only women he's ever known that doesn't mind him smoking occasionally during sex rather than after. He's explained to every woman he's ever been with that this habit isn't due to some fiercely gripping addiction, but instead is a performance enhancer. He feels as though he can focus more and would, therefore, provide a richer experience. Typically this explanation is met with something like, "*No way, I'm not risking you burning me, I know how you can get.*" or "*Come on, let's just do this I need to get back home before my boyfriend gets suspicious.*"

Veronica, however, trusting Tim beyond most of her friends and families constant insistence of discretion has never really had any problems with most of Tim's quirks. Besides which, she herself has performed this strange ritual once or twice. Although, she would be the first to admit, it never really seemed to make any difference.

WHITE NOISE (AND BLACK MATTER)

■ 12:30AM AUGUST 21ST 1985

The Quartz closes at one am, Sunday through Wednesday and probably could have closed earlier this night as the crowd had mostly dissipated by eight or so. But Eddie, unlike his father, insists the bar have a set schedule as a courtesy to its patrons, there is nothing he hates more than businesses that feel as though they can open and close whenever they so desire yet they proceed to complain, at any given moment, because they have no steady customer base. This was the case with The Quartzsite Bar when it was run by Eddie's father Richard. Richard would often close earlier in the day or open later at night, and on several occasions, he would not open the bar at all in accordance with his many mood swings and what both Eddie and Tim both referred to as the drunkard's ambition.

Eddie, at times, felt sickened with his father's handling of the family business, and knew that he was best suited on the patron's side of the bar. This sentiment could only be all but confirmed when Richard, in a drunken fit late one night in May, nineteen seventy-eight, plowed his car into a juniper tree not far up the road from The Quartzsite Bar. By the time the fire was extinguished, very little of what remained of the fifty-seven year old man could be identified.

The Quartz was closed only once since the accident, on the day of Richard's funeral, partially to acknowledge the memory of its previous owner but mostly because, even though at times

Eddie and Tim may have been short on respect for their father, they had no real reason not to love him and appreciated that he'd always at least tried to offer paternal support.

The only other bar in the town, Speedy's, remained open and saw a momentary increase in its amount of drinking crowds that day. A longtime friend of the family, Speedy opened his bar, with a considerable donation from Richard, around ten years before the brothers revived The Quartzsite Bar. And as less of a competitor and more of a sister company, partially due to Speedy's location being on the opposite side of town, Speedy and Richard would regularly visit, and later stumble out of, one another's bars.

The night of the funeral Eddie and Tim both came very close to joining their father in an almost identical event after they had spent a large remainder of the night at Speedy's. Luckily, there were no junipers around Speedy's, and both Tim and Eddie managed only to total Eddie's car in a wash. In response to their survival, they received inspiration and decided to 'fell the beast' that claimed their father and resolved to cut down the juniper tree. This was considered favorable for business as they'd be removing an obstacle that could potentially reduce repeat business. After walking back into the bar they convinced Michael to drive them to the now infamous location to commit the drunken deed with an old chainsaw they'd stolen a few hours earlier from somebody's pickup parked at the bar. And, needless to say to anybody who had seen Eddie or Tim that night, the following day would be the only day The Quartz opened later than the regular ten am schedule.

From that night on, about thirty feet from the Quartz left-side parking lot could be found a juniper stump with the name Richard Chapel followed by '1921 – 1978' carved into its center.

Tim and Veronica finish tabulating all of the receipts and tickets and Tim places the record charts along with the cash into the safe. Tim proceeds to clean the bar as Veronica finishes bussing and cleaning the tables.

"I guess I'll be driving you home." Veronica calls out to Tim as she turns the 'closed' sign.

"Yeah, I'd hoped so. My legs are killing me from standing around all damn day; don't think I could make it walking back to my apartment." Tim grabs the radios behind the bar and stuffs them in his two front pockets.

"What's that? Oh it's that walkman you bought."

"Yeah, and Gramps gave me his old Regency radio, it works alright, but honestly, I doubt I'll ever use it, the Walkman's got much better sound. Didn't have the heart to turn him down, and besides, it may be worth some money someday." Tim takes a drag of his last cigarette and places it in the ashtray, still smoking.

Veronica removes her waitress apron and takes a seat at the bar. She watches as Tim mops the floors, as sloppily as the task could possibly be accomplished.

"That's a real interesting story, Tim. Hurry up with that." Finishing what remains of Tim's cigarette, Veronica stamps the butt and returns it to the tray.

"Why don't you go do the dishes, 'stead of sitting around— that was my last cigarette, by the way, you lazy mooch."

"I still have a pack, sucker, keep your pants on."

Veronica stands and pats her back pocket where she keeps her pack of smokes. Tim swears for a second that she gropes her butt cheek while patting, but dismisses the thought. As she retreats to the back to clean the dishes, she taunts Tim with her most seductive hip-swinging walk. She stops, kisses the air and winks at him. He's now certain she groped her butt cheek; she's toying with him.

"Ah damn, Ronnie...what the hell are you trying to do me? I just spilled the bucket all over the place."

"I told you...hurry up." Veronica uses her most alluring voice as she disappears into the back room.

Tim joins Veronica in the back room shortly after mopping up all the excess water he'd used previously to flood the bar both with and without intent. Grabbing Veronica around the waist he kisses her neck as she lifts and tilts her head affectionately upwards inviting him to continue. He grabs her left butt cheek, gropes for a second and pulls out her cigarettes.

"That's what I was looking for. Thanks, Babe."

"Funny guy, hurry up and take out the trash."

With a few quick motions Tim lights up a cigarette and places his lighter and Veronica's soft pack into his front shirt pocket. He grabs the garbage bag out of the can and the bag set beside it that must have been relaxing in that same slumped position since earlier in the day.

"Why the hell didn't Eddie take this one out? Bastard. It wasn't even that busy today."

"Stop complaining and hurry up." Veronica washes her hands and returns to the bar with the newly cleaned dishes stacked on a tray.

Freeing his right hand of the garbage and stench-laden bag, Tim opens the back door. He returns the second garbage bag into his right and walks out, not once touching the cigarette in his mouth, which is now begging to be ashed. He drops the bags by the stoop perched before the door and sits on the cheap, greasy black mat that lay slowly decaying on the stoop. Reaching into his front jean pocket, Tim leans back to his left and allows easy access to his otherwise tight pocket. The old Regency radio, once tightly ensnared within the jean pocket is freed and allowed to bear witness, once more, to the open air. Tim fiddles with the antenna; straightening and extending it and then turns the radio's power knob. It screeches, emitting an almost unbearable sound that resembles a combination of high pitched white noise, steady beating electrostatic pulses, and a strange low toned growl that seems to echo. Tim quickly shuts the radio off, places the antenna back in its original position and stuffs the radio back into its pocket prison.

"Piece of shit."

Tim grumbles and stands up retrieving the garbage bags. As he heads to the dumpster behind the bar, the light flickers and dims slightly. Looking up Tim squints and snarls.

"Just got through replacing the wiring for that fucking thing!"

Turning back to the dumpster, he drops a bag on the ground to free a hand and open the garbage lid.

With the dumpster's location secured firmly along the back wall that shares the now dimmed light, there is little illumination reaching into the interior of the dumpster. This, coupled with the shadow of the lid, make it virtually impossible for Tim to make out any detail as to the contents of the garbage container. Tim knows, however, with reason, that he never really had the desire to see the contents of this or any other dumpster. And with that thought, he throws the first bag into the dumpster. He then reaches down and picks up the last bag hoisting it over his right side and drops it in beside the other garbage bag.

"Shit."

Tim realizes that he just dropped his cigarette in with the second bag. He considers leaving it but realizes that with its still lit, it could pose an issue when the cigarette is introduced to the random paper, plastic, and alcohol covered contents of The Quartz' city supplied dumpster.

Leaning over the front side of dumpster he reaches in blindly, hoping his hand, while groping around, will meet his cigarette, but not be burned by the reunion. Instead, his hand meets something else entirely. At first the sensation of the material he touches invokes a mental image of some warm pudding that is much thicker and probably older than it should be. This sensation is instantly defeated with what Tim would call a searing, and unbelievable pain. It feels as though something is burning away the flesh of his hand all the while grinding into his bones with thousands of tiny and incredibly sharp teeth. Of course, his instinctive reaction clicks in with less than a millisecond to spare as Tim attempts to jerk his hand away, if only to find a devoured stump of bone lightly dashed with traces of flesh and blood.

However, as much as he tries to withdraw his hand, Tim is unsuccessful. He cannot remove it and responds with even greater forceful tugs, but his struggle is in vain. Whatever has taken hold of him will not let go for the world, not for the universe, not for anything. In fact, as Tim struggles against the material that could only be described as some kind of black, living, otherworldly and glutinous mass, the apparent response is even greater pain and violent jerks as if hundreds of thousands of powerful little hooks are being yanked and ripped through his hand and arm. For every centimeter he might have managed to pull back the viscous tar doubles its reach across his arm. And it does so as if it is crawling along with the use of its digging teeth-like protrusions as its only means for traction.

Although to Tim it would be nearly an eternity of skirmishing between him and his dark nemesis, it is merely a matter of but a few seconds before Tim's body is completely engulfed up to his right leg. This leg, he swings down into the front rim of the dumpster with as much strength as he can muster, digging his heel into the rim. After trying to hook his heel over the rim in an attempt to pull his body towards the front of the dumpster he only manages to pull off and drop his shoe onto the asphalt underneath the garbage container.

Within an instant Tim is completely hidden somewhere within the tar, which in a few short moments following begins devouring itself. It seems the mass of molten gob has acquired its only needed victim and no longer feels the need to stick around. It manages the same wriggling and crawling motion over its own remains and quickly, fluidly overlaps and surges violently over its own form several times until it, too, disappears.

THE TROUBLE WITH TIM (BAD SNEAKERS)

■ 2:15AM AUGUST 21ST 1985

Lying uncovered in his hole-pocked underwear on his bed beside, and possibly too close to his wife, Eddie sweats to the incredibly uncomfortable, muggy, and sweltering 106 degree weather that summers in Bowling are infamous for. His cooling system has been in and out the entire month. Eddie had asked Mike, the wizard of all things mechanical and electrical, to take a look at his cooler motor several times over the past few weeks, Mike finally agreed to do so Monday, assuring Eddie he would be out to fix it, but wouldn't be available until after his vacation. In the meantime, Mike gave Eddie his high powered, water-cooled, window box fan, which ultimately only succeeds in needlessly blowing and shifting the parching air.

Eddie flips his pillow over for the fortieth time in an attempt to cool his head with the side that hasn't recently absorbed all of his body heat, and in just three seconds the 'cool' side can't rightfully be referred to as such. Jill is also uncovered, wearing only her undergarment, which happens to be a very alluring and provocative piece of black lingerie. This is because, after they returned home from the movies, the Chapels had additional plans for the night. They have only been married for two years, but have been trying frequently and fervently to have their first child. Given that Jill was ovulating, and Eddie had some time to relax, it seemed it could be a fruitful night—albeit a short one.

Jill rolls over and clasps her arms around Eddie's chest and wraps her legs around his. This is all Eddie needs; another body meshing its ninety-eight point six degree heat with his. He tries to gently remove himself from the now accursed grip of his wife's body, but only manages to free his arms and a leg. He lays there in quiet frustration staring desperately at the ceiling, hoping morning will come soon.

The phone rings.

Eddie reaches over to his nightstand and picks it up.

"Hello?!"

Eddie is not awoken by the call but maintains the sound of drowsiness for the sake of producing the guise of one who has just been abruptly ripped from the realm of deep slumber. Maybe, hopefully, he would have the opportunity to vent his current frustrations out onto the stupid asshole who feels the need to call him at two in the morning. He instantly thinks of Tim.

"Tim's missing."

It apparently isn't Tim on the other side of the phone; the voice wistfully assures Eddie of this through the ear piece.

"He left to the take the trash outside, I went out to look for him after about fifteen minutes because he hadn't come back in and I can't find him. I was supposed to drive him home and I've looked everywhere for him, but he's gone!"

"It's alright Ronnie, calm down. How long has it been since you last saw him?" Eddie uses two fingers to gently massage the weary space between his eyes.

"Over an hour, but I looked all around the bar, even drove around the block, he's not anywhere. I found his shoe by the dumpster—I thought for a second, I don't even want to say it, but I opened the dumpster and looked in, from what I could see it was completely empty, I even put my arm down in to feel if there was anything there, but it's completely empty. No garbage, no bags; not even the ones Tim was carrying out. I didn't hear him yell or anything. I don't know—"

"Don't jump to any conclusions, he's probably just screwing with you. You know as well as I do." Eddie thinks for a moment about the dumpster, it was almost full before he left his shift.

"What's going on Eddie?" A dreary eyed Jill leans up over Eddie trying to read his face.

He holds his hand over the phone mic.

"It's Ronnie, she can't find Tim." He smiles trying to show that there is no need for concern, but Jill, quite capable of reading Eddie like a book, detects his uneasiness.

"I thought about that Eddie, but that's a long time for a stupid prank. I probably don't need to tell you...but I'm worried, I think something's wrong. Should I call the police?" Ronnie speaks through weighted tears and increasing frustration.

"I don't know, they won't do much if it's only been an hour, but I get you, it is strange. Look, I'm going to head out here, I'll be there in about ten, fifteen minutes. I'll keep an eye out on my way there. But, don't worry Ronnie, we'll find Tim. I'm sure he's fine. Try to stay calm and I'll be right over."

Eddie hangs up the phone and grabs his pants lying near the bed.

"How long has he been gone?" Jill too starts dressing.

"Probably about an hour and a half, she said his shoe was lying on the ground next to the dumpster which was completely empty?"

Again, the peculiarity of this thought strikes Eddie. *Why the hell would someone empty the dumpster*?

"He was taking out the trash and disappeared, I guess. If it *is* a joke I'm gonna kick his ass."

What sort of joke would that be? Eddie thinks for a moment then grabs his keys and puts his arms around his wife.

"You don't need to come, I'll be alright, and I'll let you know what's going on."

"Tim's my brother too, besides...it's too hot to sleep."

"Yeah, no kidding. *Damned Mike*." Eddie mutters these last two words with a slight exasperation.

He kisses Jill and holds her hands for a moment staring deeply into her eyes. She can see that he is troubled, but also appears to be very fixated on something.

"What are you thinking?" Jill leans into Eddie and tries her most calming voice.

"Ah, nothing...I think it's just shaping up to be an unusual week. You know Gramps' dog went missing earlier today—not that it means anything but...It's weird right?"

"I guess. Stranger things have happened." Jill smirks and lightly pecks Eddie's cheek.

Ronnie sits at the bar drinking a cup of black coffee; fiddling her hands which seem to be at a greater loss than she. This is the kind of time when Ronnie typically finds she could really, really use a cigarette.

No kidding, where'd you take my cigarettes Tim?

Her hands seem to express agreement; trying desperately to defeat their anxiety and frustration usually subsided by the near constant grasp of a soothing cigarette. Were her boyfriend not missing with her pack, she would likely not need them so ardently. She reaches across the bar top, grabbing the bottle of whiskey she'd set on the counter moments before and pours enough into her coffee that the black actually begins to delude. No cream, no sugar, just black coffee and Southern Comfort.

Ronnie had stopped crying since she'd spoken with Eddie on the phone, but has made no efforts to fix her eyeliner and mascara now forming coarse, dark trails along her flushed cheeks. After pushing her hands through her hair, as she leans her head down with closed eyes, she blows out a sigh and purses her lips.

She sips her coffee and quietly waits staring at the front of her mug which features a blue cartoon cat with a thought bubble encircling the words *'Mondays are alright with a good cup of Joe!'*. A gift from Tim, who'd found the cartoon, in relation to Veronica's penchant for coffee, particularly amusing.

Veronica shakes her head and looks to the neon shapes along the wall in an attempt to distract her thoughts.

■ 2:40AM

The Chapels arrive at The Quartz; Eddie unlocks the door and steps in to find Ronnie dozing at the bar.

"Hey Ronnie, wake up honey. How are you holding up?" Jill gently nudges Ronnie awake.

"I'm fine, I kind of feel stupid for calling you guys, I mean it could be nothing, like you said. It just seemed really strange, and I've never felt a sinking feeling like that before."

Eddie doesn't speak because he too can feel that same sort of dread Ronnie speaks of, and though Ronnie seems to have calmed, he himself can't shake the feeling. It isn't death that's caught his mind, but something just as troubling and much less explainable. Without a word, Eddie heads quickly to the back door as Ronnie and Jill watch the strange, fixated and uneasy movement he exhibits.

"It's always night time when stuff like this happens." Jill looks to Veronica with a smile and an attempt at alleviation.

"Of course."

Veronica responds in kind, but neither finds much success in the daunting atmosphere Eddie unintentionally creates.

Opening the door to the back alley behind The Quartz, Eddie flips on the light. It flickers for a moment and beams on; completely illuminating the alley, the dumpster and all within immediate sight. Slowly walking around the dumpster perched against the wall, Eddie closely examines the contents of the container as had been done repeatedly several times through-out the day. However, it now acts indifferently to any logical assumption suggested countless hours before, as sure enough, it is completely empty. Eddie closes the lid and for a quick sec-ond feels an incredible burning sensation in his hand grasping around the garbage lid. He jerks it back to look at his hand and sees nothing out of the ordinary.

At this same moment with Eddie's attention focused entirely on his hand, the remnants of the black material dissipate from the lid, as if having remained for those couple of hours merely waiting for Eddie to ensure he experiences what could only amount to a minute percentage of what his brother felt only a short time before. It sparks a curiosity in Eddie that forces him to again closely examine the lid and the interior of the dumpster. What he finds, astoundingly, is nothing. Nothing is astounding because it implies that not only is the interior of the dumpster wiped clean of its various deep stains previously teeming with bacteria, but that the permanent splotch of what once was a very poorly constructed and especially starchy fettuccine is now completely erased from the steel walls of the garbage container. In fact, if the walls could speak they may be inclined to sing, as the presence of clean is so strong, they likely have no recollection of ever being so incredibly filthy.

After touching and caressing the metal in disbelief Eddie once again closes the lid. He hesitates for a moment and tries to envision scenarios in which this could make sense—and draws a complete blank. To Eddie, this makes no sense at all, and is therefore cause for some alarm. Eddie reenters The Quartz and walks back into the bar. Quietly, he sits down beside his wife and massages his own hand staring at it in deep fixation.

"I didn't find anything, but it's like you said, it doesn't make sense." Eddie remarks in quite bemusement and scratches his neck.

"Jill, why don't you head home? You too, Ronnie, I'll hang out here, I've slept in the back before, I have an old cot and a sleeping bag somewhere in the storage back there. I'll wait around for Tim and let you know if he shows up."

Eddie lifts his hand and turns it slowly allowing the shadows to be chased away by the bar lights. He closes it and returns it to the bar top.

"If not...I don't know, I guess I'll call the police in the morning and find out what they think we should do. It hasn't been long enough, really, to even be worried. I'm worried too...but this is Tim we're talking about." Eddie smiles to his wife and friend, trying at the very least, to inject some cheer into the situation.

"I mean the guy's always out with Mike. God only knows what kind of shit he's gotten into at one time or another, he'll probably show up with some crazy ass story...who knows, I say we just take it easy and wait—do you have that shoe?"

Veronica reaches under her barstool and tosses the sneaker.

"Oh, you need the keys?" Eddie pulls them from his pocket and makes a motion preparing to toss them to Jill.

"I'll give her a ride home. She doesn't want to drive that boat of yours." Ronnie smiles, lifts her purse over her shoulder and winks at Jill knowing she secretly detests Eddie's second love.

Referring to the heavy, powerful, and large 1962 Pontiac Catalina 421 Super Duty Eddie has driven since he'd totaled his car outside of Speedy's. Consequently, Speedy, who received his nickname due to his hobby of collecting and racing new and old performance vehicles, was the man who'd sold the vehicle to the eldest Chapel brother at a greatly discounted price of $1,800. He'd later sold the youngest brother a 1979 Pontiac Firebird for around the same price. Speedy was considered to be like an uncle to the two Chapel brothers and was always trusted to cut them a break or lend them a hand, as their father had often done for Speedy.

Though both brothers greatly prized the vehicles, their significant others were always less than enthusiastic with their choices and the resulting attachment. In some ways, this as-sisted in helping to form the bond between Veronica and Jill, as more often than not, when participating in outings with the

Chapel brothers they would share Ronnie's more sensible Volvo and let the boys play with the childish things they never seemed likely to put aside.

■ 4:21 AM

Eddie lies in his sleeping bag with his arms crossed behind his head staring at the ceiling of the small office room built behind the back corner of the bar. He turns and stares in the low light at Tim's shoe lying on his office desk. It's a beat up old white pump with bits of red and white on the side, likely a knock-off brand, as Tim would rarely spend more than $20 on any article of clothing. Somehow, this thought caught Eddie. Tim was typically cheap when it came to spending for himself, but with most anyone else he seemed to have no spending limit, and would especially fork out any amount for Ronnie. Now depressed, Eddie considers for a moment, that this shoe may be the last piece of Tim he ever sees, this bad sneaker, worn far past its prime. He figures this must've been a similar thought to one Gramps formed when staring at the remnants of Pete's collar.

Eddie shoots up out of the sleeping bag and sits for a moment, rubbing his hands into his face. He grabs the touch tone phone and dials 9-1-1.

"Hello, I'd like to report a missing person."

The dispatcher clearly sighs and mumbles; "No way, not another one."

She then speaks up.

"I'll need a few things. Who is it that's missing, where are you, where is, I mean, where was the missing person when he or she was last seen?"

Though they operated a popular social lounge, in a not so popular town, there were very few occasions when Eddie and Tim needed to call the police for assistance, as they had a tendency to deal with their issues in a more vigilante manner.

But the few times that required such assistance created a some-what undesired familiarity with the often tactless and flakey dispatcher.

"Hi Julie, its Eddie. Tim is missing, he's been missing since around 1:00 this morning. Thing is, he was covering my shift with Ronnie. She says he went outside to take the trash out before they shut down the bar and he hasn't shown up since... By the way, what do you mean another one? Has this been happening a lot lately?"

"I don't know if I should say anything Ed, but we've got twelve missing persons, *twelve*, if you can believe that. One of them is Officer James. Last night he left Speedy's. Speedy said he saw him walk out, and that was the last anybody's seen of him. The bodies gotta be piling up *somewhere*."

Eddie would like to remark but instead holds his tongue, realizing these kind of comments are likely to continue with or without his input.

"I guess Speedy thought he heard gun shots, ran outside and James was gone, but you're brother had plowed into his light pole, he said. Don't worry though, he said it was no big deal, or nothin', it wasn't the first time somebody's done that—any-ways, I guess that's the least of Tim's worries now." Julie pauses and realizes, surprisingly to anyone familiar with the woman, how her words could be construed as a callused remark.

"Sorry Eddie, geez, I don't why I said that, that came out totally wrong—"

"Don't worry about it...I don't know, doesn't this all strike you as strange?" Eddie considers for a moment the absurdity of this question; a minimal amount of subjects would likely phase or even register with, the stunningly naïve dispatcher.

"Anyway, I didn't know if I should report it yet, it could be nothing, but I guess something really is going on."

Eddie anxiously fidgets with the phone cord stretching it out between his fingers and subsiding several of the curls.

"With a missing person report, the sooner the better. So...is that all you know? What about Ronnie? Did she see anything?"

"That's all we know really. She found his shoe by the dumpster, that's it."

"And the dumpster...you searched it? I mean, you don't want to think about it, but maybe someone hit him and dumped his body in there." This comment does not strike the macabre Julie as a poor choice in words as had her previous statement.

Eddie shakes his head. He had always considered it a strange decision when the precinct hired Julie as a dispatcher, he supposed it had something to do with her child-like reasoning and how in some strange way, it imposed an amount of lightheartedness into an otherwise troubling occupation.

"Yeah, Ronnie and I both did. I think she had the same thought. She even searched around the block a few times. Nothing. He's just gone."

Julie responds despondently; "Hopefully just missing and not—Well, I'll get the word out Eddie, I mean he could be okay, you know but, there's been so many of these cases coming in, who knows what we'll be able—"

"Yeah, look, I've got to head out and check in on Jill and Ronnie. Let me know what you hear." Eddie masks his frustration to an extent but allows Julie to receive the hint of dissatisfaction.

"Sorry Eddie, we'll do what we can."

Julie seems to be trailing off as if losing interest in the conversation in response to something occurring in her immediate surroundings.

Eddie hangs up.

After filling a travel mug found in the office with some piping hot and incredibly strong coffee, composed of approximately seven tablespoons of grounds for a twenty ounce travel mug, Eddie opens the door and is met with the Arizona morning sunrise. He finds his Catalina where he'd left it earlier and in the morning haze, fumbles for his keys in his right front pocket.

Eddie ensures the tape deck's volume is set to a just-below-blaring level and blasts the album he had just received a month before as a thirty-sixth birthday gift from his brother; a fittingly titled Dire Straits' album, "Brothers in Arms", as he takes off with Tim's shoe perched tightly between the windshield and the dash.

The Chapel homestead is a two-story house located on Seventh and Saguaro, roughly five miles from The Quartz. With the growing trend of postmodern architecture and given that the Georgian style of Eddie's house was something of a rarity in Arizona, the house demanded attention proclaiming a presence nearly as prevalent as his bar. The plus side to this; the house is very easy to find on drunken nights or on weary sleepless mornings.

As Eddie pulls into his driveway, he is not surprised to see Ronnie's small red car blocking the path to his garage. He figured she would stay with Jill, as the thoughts of Tim he fought in solitude throughout the hours, could only have been worse for her. And, as is often the case, the best solution would be to remain in the company of friends or family. Being honest with himself, Eddie admits that he should have done the same, as he is feeling more depressed now than he has in several years. As he walks through the door, he finds Ronnie asleep on the pullout sofa, with Jill passed out on the other three-piece couch that composes the living set found in the entrance room of their house. He would have wondered why one of them hadn't simply used the bed, were it not for the few bottles of wine positioned randomly on the coffee table. He proceeds quietly to the kitchen and makes another pot of coffee.

Eddie sits for some time at the kitchen table with somber resolve consuming what must be his third cup of coffee, excluding the travel mug. He stops and holds his face with one hand staring into his mug as the sugar he pours dissolves, thinking deeply, or at least as deeply as could be managed with the tremendous amounts of caffeine now coursing through his body.

Tim, Pete, and God knows who else. Had they died...is Tim dead? If not, what the hell happened to them? And what the hell is that black tar?

Though Eddie hadn't yet seen the already legendary black tar, drawing lines between points, he builds a connection.

Fuck Tim, where the hell are you?

Jill can feel her shoulder being forced gently forward, repeatedly. She struggles to open her eyes, but feels herself succumb to a sensation of paralysis, and after a few moments of trying to wake, she dozes off again. Eddie hesitates and then turns Jill over to face him sitting over her body on the couch. "Jill! Wake up!" This time Eddie clasps both shoulders and lightly shakes her body.

Jill blearily opens her eyes.

"I think I'm going to go looking for Tim." Eddie says earnestly.

"What?"

Jill sits up stretching and yawning with a fairly frustrated look on her face.

"What do you mean, just drive around looking for him? Didn't you do that already? Did you call the police?"

"Yes, I called them. They won't be able to do anything... they've been getting multiple missing person reports daily. Tim is just one of many now."

Looking to Ronnie, Eddie sees that she, too, is awake as she turns to face them.

"What about the bar?" She asks.

"I'll call Speedy and see if he can look after things while I'm gone. Or you could bartend..." Eddie had already planned these details throughout the sleepless night, and had, in the back of his mind, the strange inclination that he may not be returning to Bowling, let alone The Quartz.

"Oh no, if you're going looking for Tim, so am I. I want nothing to do with The Quartz, if you guys aren't there."

Ronnie smiles and awaits commentary.

Eddie had assumed this would be Veronica's response.

He turns to Jill as she tilts her head, shrugging her shoulders. He takes it as both an agreement and a blessing.

WHEREABOUTS UNKNOWN
(OBSCURED BY CLOUDS)

Tim is not dead.

"Shit, I wish I was."

Tim mutters these words in response to what he likens to a hangover; the worst hangover he's ever had. Wanting to lie motionless with his eyes closed, Tim fears that any change may erupt in sharp, powerful pains screaming through his head. He vaguely remembers what should have been only moments ago. He can't have a hangover; he hasn't had anything to drink for some time. Remembering the occurrence with the dumpster, Tim decides he should be dead. However, considering that he is not in fact dead, Tim realizes it may be best to try to get a grip on things, and perhaps prove with the utmost certainty that he has not yet passed away.

"What the hell just happened?" Tim finds himself straining his voice into a murmur once again and struggles to open his eyes. He manages, and looks forward with the ground running parallel to the left side of his vision. He can't move and lies still, waiting for his eyes to focus through the pain streaming through his nasal tracks and behind his eyes, hoping sight might help make some sense of what had just occurred.

It doesn't.

In fact, Tim currently despises his ability to see, and quickly closes his eyes. Nothing is right with what he had just witnessed.

In the few seconds he'd kept his eyes open, Tim perceived a vast desert of red-orange sand and stone, with large spires and monoliths bearing crooked, unearthly shapes in the distance. As if the scene were formed from some great, violent corrosion happening too suddenly to allow the masses of objects remaining to settle with time.

These formations are set against a dark amaranthine sky, studded endlessly with bright stars pulsing and gleaming through great, quick moving clouds that travel vertically; adverse to the obscured horizon with an apparent contempt to any natural laws Tim thought he knew.

With his eyes still closed, Tim rolls over unto his stomach and forces his hands under his chest. Pushing forward with his arms and planting his feet into the strangely soft, malleable soil, Tim manages to set himself unto a standing position, albeit an awkward, swaggering and unsure one.

After standing with his eyes closed for one painstaking minute, the pain in his head seems to melt down through his body before completely disappearing.

He opens his eyes.

With this second bout of sightseeing, the clouds are moving even faster than before and through the clouds he can see a large blue moon split by the toothy horizon, accompanied by a smaller but brighter silvery green moon, or possibly a planet. It certainly looks more like a planet, at least like pictures of planets Tim vaguely recalls seeing pinned to walls in the junior high school science classrooms.

He looks down at his feet, suddenly made aware of his missing shoe. He lifts his foot and flexes his toes; one manages to escape the surly bonds of sock to bask in the somehow orange glow cast over everything within sight.

Tim observes his shadow cast before him and surmises that the light being shone upon the ground is emitting from somewhere above him, and as he cranes his head skywards, Tim finds a large orange star peering over the great landscape.

He lifts his arm to shield his eyes in the shadow cast.

The sky is teeming with its own, very unfamiliar biology. What look to be thousands of long, but very minute cylindrical creatures flying with several twisting wings that appear to be rotating around their bodies, swim in fluid and precise motion as they tear quickly through the sky. The swarming organisms appear to encompass a great stretch of the open air, and off in the distance, distorted by the clouds of these otherworldly bugs, Tim can make out two or three large floating shapes that at first glance, remind him of trees uprooted and slowly swimming in the air with limbs flailing downwards like tentacles. Only rather than foliage at the top, great bulbous mushroom-like growths provide the canopy for these massive floating creatures.

The ground, however, is vast and empty like a great valley of red desert surrounded by the oddest looking mountains and stone arcs Tim has ever seen. Wafting through the mountains in the distance below the swarms and hovering fungal growths is a thin green and grey fog blanketing a small area suspended just above the horizon. Because this fog is moving at an incredibly sluggish rate, it appears almost rigid. He considers it similar to seeing Bryce National Park after eating half an ounce of peyote, a practice with which Tim had become familiarized not long after graduating high school, when he used the school-free time to depart on camping excursions with his dropout buddy Michael. Though he always remembers these moments fondly, he does not remember them clearly.

Tim pats his chest, and sighs in relief when his hand meets his, or rather, Veronica's pack of cigarettes. He places a cigarette between his lips and retrieves Ronnie's lighter. Cupping his hand around the lighter and cigarette he takes a puff. The taste of the tobacco seems much more concentrated and richer than he remembers with the last cigarette he'd smoked; what would have been, in his mind, only moments ago. He even coughs; a reaction a single drag has not been potent enough to cause in many years.

With the remarkably strong cigarette still in his mouth Tim stops and considers his surroundings momentarily, then shakes his head clear of the daze and with the cigarette bouncing to a single syllable Tim poses a thousand statements and questions; all at once.

"Fuck?!"

And with this word a trail of smoke cautiously escapes his mouth into an unwelcoming and unyielding alien sky.

Coincidentally, at the same instant Tim utters what is perhaps the most bewildered word of his life; Pete awakens in a small dark crater, turns his head towards the same sky and peering through the vast shadow of the eastern rim of a now encompassing crater, howls maliciously in frustration at a large unsettling moon.

If a dog's brain could comprehend the sophisticated structuring of the English language, or any human language for that matter, and sift through the thousands of words available, Pete's howl would transmogrify into a choice statement describing every emotion he is currently experiencing. His muzzle and tongue would force together into a movement appropriate to form the single word; 'Thuck!' Which would mean 'Fuck!', but because the dog is incapable of moving his bottom lip in a manner required to form the 'F' sound, this would be the greatest attempt Pete could make.

Unlike Tim, however, Pete does not really question his predicament, nor does he question his surroundings. He has grown accustomed to his inability to control certain things in life, but he also realizes that he does not, by any means, have to accept it as inevitable, and with that thought he speeds up the western side of the crater in a valiant attempt to mount the rim.

He does not.

Instead, he loses footing, aslips and spirals down into the center of the large depression. Sitting for a moment, he ponders deeply, considering the formation of the land around him, determining the velocity and speed required to achieve success and with one more burst of determination he attempts the climb again.

And again, he fails.

After further consideration, Pete realizes that due to his lacking the necessary strength to achieve the require speed, coupled with the overall scale and general grade of the rim of the crater, he simply cannot surmount it.

He tries once more; just the same.

■ UNKNOWN DATE AND TIME
(ONE MINUTE LATER THAN BEFORE)

"Sounded like a dog." Tim is comforted somewhat by the sheer normalcy of this thought.

He begins to walk westward believing he is walking in the direction of the howling he heard a minute ago. Why he is walking in that direction, is not entirely clear to him. Of course, what could be waiting for him when he finds the source of the howl may not be a dog at all; instead, it may be something monumental, predatory, horrific and caustic in its very appearance. It may also have a particular lack in fondness for the human race, and upon first sight may decide, though Tim, in his foreign nature, is detestable in appearance, he may yet be quite delectable in taste.

However, as it stands, Tim has no other bearings to choose from, and the howl discharges through the cliffs and along the sands as a familiar sound in completely unfamiliar surroundings.

After walking a half of a mile, Tim is stirred by several high-pitched peals accompanied by waves of low toned garbling noises he recognizes to be similar to the rhythmic radio static he had once heard before; just before the unspeakably bizarre experience. Remembering the two radios stuffed in both pockets, Tim reaches first for the Regency as his right side bears more of the vibration generated by sound. It is, as he assumed, the Regency emanating the static though under no recollection of his own had he switched the radio power dial. Yet as if in complete disregard to Tim's wishes; it is powered and working very diligently to introduce loud noise into an otherwise quiet moment.

He fiddles with the tuner and volume only to find that it makes absolutely no difference and the steady flow of noise remains completely uninterrupted and unchanged. Tim then decides the pulsing signals are far too obnoxious and turns the radio off. Much to Tim's surprise the radio suddenly becomes obedient and yields, leaving only the subtle wails, murmurs and flits of the atmosphere surrounding the radio-bearing biped.

Before he begins again, Tim surveys his surroundings once more and tries to keep in mind the general direction in which he has been traveling. Not much has changed in terms of scenery, and any visible landmarks are positioned at too great of a distance to be of much use outside of broad, generalized compass directions.

He looks instead, to the sandy flooring around him and notices in the area to his left, a small depression about six feet across. It is filled to the brim with the malicious black substance that had devoured him only hours ago. Carefully, and with stupid curiosity, he walks towards the cavity and stares deeply into the tar. It seems featureless as it moves and crawls slowly within and upon itself, it doesn't even catch a shine as if light cannot touch it. Tim notices, after a few seconds, that the pool of malcontent is moving faster and concentrates itself towards the side of the cavity nearest his position. It appears as if Tim would again be the focus of these unearthly organisms' appetites.

Tim reaches down and retrieves a small red rock and tosses it into the pool. Reacting instantly and aggressively in a barrage of quickly multiplied and fierce movements focused almost entirely around the area where the rock made contact with the obsidian surface.

The rock didn't have a fighting chance, though it did fight, admirably and with a great, steady strength, as rocks often do.

"Sayonara." Tim says and follows with a quick shutter as he is immediately reminded of the worst pain he'd ever experienced in his still young life. Now bored and somewhat disturbed by the black puddle he turns to leave, continuing in the direction he'd been sure to make a mental note of.

■ 10:10PM AUGUST 11TH 2009
(TANGENTIAL SPACE/TIME)

Just behind an aging Mars rover currently scouring the cold and dusty terrain of the red Martian surface, a small pool of black tar spews forth a rock unlike anything the planet has ever encountered. The stone travels one foot before smashing into the hull of the rover causing its computers to reboot.

The rock then, as if evading the crawling robot, ricochets and returns to the swarthy substance which quickly devours itself dissolving into infinite time and space.

The rover continues forward shortly afterwards to search for signs of life with the application of geological surveys conducted across the defunct planet.

■ UNKNOWN DATE AND TIME
(LESS THAN ONE HOUR LATER)

Another mile slowly builds in tedium and desolation behind Tim before he sees yet another cavity in the short distance ahead of him. A large crater becomes his point of focus as he quickens his pace, if only to hurry to his death. But, at this point, Tim welcomes any change with excitement; although it could bring death, it could also bring help, or even answers. The thought of change itself is now enticing. The questions and deliberations, of course, remain the same, and could still be summed up in the intelligibly gifted and eloquent manner

Tim has already conveyed. Except that now *'Fuck?!'* could also mean: *What's in this crater? Is there really a dog somewhere on this planet? Maybe the dog's in the crater. Maybe someone's in the crater with the dog. Maybe they could help. Maybe they know what's going on.* Lastly, as Tim stomach is beginning to insist; *"I'm fuckin' hungry."*

This last sentiment Tim decides to vocally announce for no other reason than the simple fact that this is all he usually would have to say before someone then replies with; *'Me too, we should stop somewhere'.* Or *'Alright, what do you want to eat?'*

Not this time.

This time the reply is a loud and excited bark, though it is possible and very likely that the bark implies the same declaration of hunger, as barks often do.

There is no question in Tim's mind now, the howling and barking he's been trying to find is coming from the crater and that it is indeed, a dog producing the sounds. In fact, Tim is certain; he's heard this dog before, which he acknowledges could be wishful thinking, but adversely insists, is not.

"Petey—PETEY, you dirty old mutt, that's gotta be you!"

Another barking reply sets Tim running towards the crater with a speed he'd never traveled by foot before. He stops just short of the crater's edge and is met with a small leaping dog which bounds up the crater's side with matching speed and launches off beyond the edge head-first into Tim's gut. Tim falls back clutching Pete as he slobbers and licks excitedly, baptizing Tim's face in welcomed dog drool.

DESERT ROADS
(JUST ANOTHER DAY ON EARTH)

■ 4:32PM AUGUST 21ST 1985

Gramps sits alone on the left side of an aging, weathered oak bench perched upon his cracked and discolored front porch. The right side of the bench had always belonged to his belated wife, Virginia, and it hadn't been used in the five years since her passing.

Gramps would like to say, as time passed, the years would fade away with greater ease, but they did not and he'd found himself just as lonely this day as he had since she'd first left.

Staring at a grouping of the dark, otherworldly matter that engulfs most of what used to be Virginia's flowerbed, Gramps thinks not only of his wife, but of his dog as well, which had only a day before faced the same fate as these unlucky petunias, daffodils, snapdragons, and orchids he'd toiled over for years in the honor of his late love.

He grimaces, grunts and retreats into his house.

A short moment later, Gramps returns to the front porch armed with a loaded twelve-gauge shotgun, and a burgeoning hatred for this dark, viscous invader.

Huffing; "Worthless pile of shit!" He blasts a round into the tarry muck.

In response, the substance gurgles, pops and swells in the numerous points of shot connection.

But it does so, not in a revelatory statement of pain, but instead in a taunting statement of disobedience. This defiance

infuriates the aged widower. But this heated fury quickly subsides and is replaced with a disheartened exhaustion. Gramps
shakes his head and sighs relieving the tensed frown in his face.
He plops himself in his bench and splits his shotgun emptying
the shells.

"What more do ya want from me? Ya got Pete...hell, Pete's
the *only* thing I got. You want my gun? Take it!"

And with this in mind Gramps finds a second wind of fury;
stands up with a grunt and hobbles until he's standing just over
the tar.

Grasping the barrel with both hands, he heaves the shotgun
above his head. In a swift and fierce motion, the aging man
swings the gun full force down into the puddle. The force is met
in kind and stops as sudden on the tar's surface as if it were a
brick wall. In an instant the muck begins climbing and pulling
quickly along the guns handle. Gramps lets go of the barrel and
falls back in revulsion.

Sitting on the soft soil, Gramps watches in awe as the tar
anxiously engulfs and feeds itself the gun. Continuing in its feast,
the blackness then devours itself and in a few short moments
disappears before the stunned elderly man.

"Eh...well, you got my gun now, too. Guess that's all I have
you wanted." Gramps achingly stands dusting off his pants seat
and grasping his hip.

Again he seats himself on the oak bench and relieves his
tired bones and muscles. He draws in a large breath and holds
it. After a few seconds he exhales through his nose, blowing
through the lazily wafting hairs in his mustache and beard.

The phone rings quietly in his house. This sends a signal
into another phone jack that traverses through a taped up wire
running along the top corners of the living room through a
small hole and out into the daylight connecting into a makeshift
alarm fashioned from a red Christmas light and an old car horn
posted just above the aging man sitting on the bench.

It lights up and sounds off familiarly saying air raid or maybe enemy approaching. In fact, sometimes the dread forced through him when hearing the phone ring caused by the anticipation of particular phone calls, could almost match the dread he'd experienced in his days as a soldier. This, however, is not one of those dreaded phone calls. Those phone calls typically come from his deadbeat nephew, who only seems to call when he is broke, homeless, and needs a place to stay, or when he has the business investment opportunity of a lifetime.

Inside of the old house, Gramps retrieves the rotary dial phone on the square end table beside his armchair.

"Damned, no good son-of-a-bitch."

He answers the phone fully prepared to give his nephew an earful.

"Hey Gramps!"

The phone peeps in a friendly voice.

"Eddie, oh hell, I thought you were gonna be Grant. Damn near chewed your ear off."

Eddie chuckles; "No such luck Gramps, you'll have to bitch him out another time—anyways, you said Pete went missing after the whole thing with the tar in your shed. I guess it's not an isolated incident, the police say there's been several missing person reports coming in."

"You talked to the cops about Pete?"

"Actually, no...that's what I'm calling for. Tim's gone missing, and I'm willing to bet whatever happened to Pete happened to Tim."

Standing in a phone booth not far from the market at the edge of the city limits, Eddie pauses and stares at the battered sneaker rotating it in his hand.

"Ah hell Eddie, that's all I needed to hear. I'm sorry."

Gramps pauses to recollect all of the information preceding this phone call and briefly ponders a few possible courses of action.

"Hell, If you find someone stupid enough to take that bet, you let me know. I wager it *is* that damned black goop doin' all of this—You tell Barb'ra?"

"Yeah, she said *'find him and bring his ass back here'.*"

Eddie mimics his mother's tone to the best of his abilities.

"You do that Eddie. Get that kid back here. I've been watching that stuff, it ain't right. It eats everything it touches and then it's gone, like it's coming here to get whatever it's lookin' for an' takes off—I don't think they're gone Eddie. I think they're just moved somewhere."

"Yeah, Gramps, I've been thinking that myself, I'm leaving town. Jill, Ronnie and I are going to look around and see if we can find that tar and maybe we can scoop it up and take it somewhere and figure out what it is, and what it's been doing. I meant to call you earlier. It's just been sort of hectic."

"I got ya Eddie, you find out what's goin' on, and find Tim... maybe then you'll even find Pete."

Gramps lands himself on his armchair and continues forming scenarios and outcomes within his mind.

"I will Gramps. I'll let you know everything I find out. Talk to you soon."

"Take it easy Eddie." Both men return their phones and Eddie leaves the phone booth. Pausing for a moment, he stares down the highway into the setting sun. Through the heat vapors rising from the pavement in the distance, Eddie can make out a single yellow pickup on the left side of the highway arriving into town.

"Mike?" Eddie wonders at the sight, considering that Mike should be at the lake and incredibly drunk, by now. Eddie, however, also regards the beat up '79 Ford as a sight for sore eyes. Mike, for his lack of wisdom, sense, punctuality and tact, could find anything and everything if only asked to do so. This in addition to his surprisingly brilliant, mechanically inclined mind could be useful in what could be an extensive search. Eddie also considers that Mike tends to, without ever really intending;

keep the mood light when needed. This is something Eddie always greatly admired about his and his brother's friend.

Mike notices Eddie, and slowing only slightly, pulls into the market parking lot just beside Eddie's car, nearly sideswiping it. Exiting the truck, Mike slams his door shut and shakes his head furiously.

"Fuck that, man...shit's way fuckin' lame!"

Responding to Mike, who appears to be upset, Eddie, now standing just beside the truck bed, interjects.

"How's the vacation going?"

"Nah, man. Fuck vacation, I'm staying indoors from now on."

Mike lifts his baseball cap and rubs his hand through his dark, thinning hair. "I left last night, right—to the lake. It was probably like one or so in the morning. I went to the north side. You remember where we tied that big-ass tractor tire to the tree?"

Yeah, it's still there?" Eddie leans on the truck and lights up a cigarette.

"Shit yeah...anyways I went there and just hung out sitting on the tailgate for a couple of minutes, then I was gonna set up a tent and everything...I see this guy a little ways off, just kind of like, shuffling around, like he was drunk or some shit. So I go walk up to him, to see if he needs help or somethin'. Make sure he doesn't drown himself in the lake. I get close to him and I'm walking up behind him. I thought maybe it was Joe, cause he's got this curly 'fro like Joe's, you know."

Mike stands staring at Eddie with a strange look watching and following his cigarette's progression from hand to mouth and back to hand with an almost longing.

"Yeah, he shaved that off though, didn't he?"

Eddie holds out his cigarette pack and with a masterful flick of the wrist causes a single cigarette to slide out from the pack.

Mike takes the offer and lights it with a Zippo that features a small embossed marijuana leaf on the side.

"Thanks."

He drags in and exhales; "Yeah, but that was a while ago, he's got it grown back now. And the guy kinda walked the same too, like his leg was all fucked up. So I get up behind him, I'm still far enough from him he can't hear my steps I guess. So I go to call his name, call 'Joe'. But then I look closer, it sure as fuck ain't Joe, dude. His ears were huge, and they looked like they were pointed. It kind of freaked me out, so I backed off a little an' I duck down behind a bush so he couldn't see me—I mean, he didn't look right."

Jill and Ronnie walk out of the market holding two bags each full of jerky, trail mix, soda, beer, sunflower seeds, bread, deli meats, various cheeses, potato chips, ranch dressing, bean dip, salsa, and potato salad; the best small town convenience store food available for a short road trip. They arrive in time to bear witness to Mike's tale, which remains on hold for the moment.

"Hey, where the fuck you guys goin' anyway?"

Mike nods at the two load-bearing women.

Feeling the stare from his wife, Eddie turns and sees them, drops his cigarette to the dirt floor and rubs his foot into it in a semicircular motion. He opens the trunk to his Catalina and positions the bags he takes from the women in a specific pattern along the trunk bed. A particular fashion that could really only make sense to him; Jill watches and shakes her head, knowing all too well, her husband's strange and sometimes obsessive idiosyncrasies.

"Thanks for the help." Jill adds in a hint of patronization as she pats her husband's back.

Eddie wraps his arm around Jill's waist as she kisses his cheek. He returns to adjusting the contents of the trunk, ensuring everything is arranged properly as he continues his conversation with Michael.

"We're actually going out to look for Tim. He disappeared last night, sometime after you left. I guess...he went out to empty the trash and never came back in. His car's still at The

Quartz. I don't know—" Eddie closes the trunk and returns to his previous position at the truck bed.

"We've been talkin' about it and think it's got something to do with whatever happened to Pete. The—"

Eddie shakes his head and gestures his hand along the ground trying to find more suitable words to portray the material Gramps had described the day before.

"Tar stuff, I guess." More suitable words slip his grasp.

"No shit, it got Tim? Fuck!"

Michael shouts and dramatically throws a stone across the street into the empty desert.

"This is bullshit, man! But—"

He leans over the open window into his truck cab and rests his upper body over crossed arms for a moment.

"Actually that's kinda where I was going with this too. At the lake, I'm hiding in the bush, right, and from behind the guy, it looks like he's holding a flashlight up to his face, you know like when you tell ghost stories or some shit. Why the fuck he would be doin' that, I don't know, but the way things were going, it wasn't like shit would be in any hurry to make sense."

Turning to face Eddie, Michael proceeds towards the climax of his story; "But then he turns around and he looked sort of normal at first, like I said, he had curly brown hair, like a 'fro, and a brown goatee, but then I stepped out over the bush a little and I can see, he doesn't have a flashlight, that light was coming from these two lit-up yellow lumps on his head."

Through the use of rudimentary gestures Mike indicates the placement of the growths; holding his hands in round shapes just above his sideburns and beside his eyebrows.

"They were like glowing lumps, like lighted tumors, but they opened and closed like they were breathing. Like fuckin' gills. An' his skin was grey, almost blue—don't laugh, but...I seriously think he was an alien."

Mike finishes his cigarette and stamps it out on the side of his Zippo before tossing it aside.

Eddie develops an intensified look of concentration and stares at Mike as Ronnie adds mockingly; "And this all happened after the thirtieth beer and two fifths of Jack."

Retreating from the vehicle window, Mike stands back and turns his face to Ronnie.

"I'll admit I was drunk. Shit, I was wasted!"

He turns and smiles at Eddie thinking he might find the statement amusing. Eddie, however, continues staring with a look implying that he is not, at the moment, mentally invested in the conversation. Mike returns to face Ronnie.

"But it's the God's honest truth what I said. And I've never been so drunk that I'm seeing shit, ask Eddie...'specially shit like that. Beer goggles only help to make heinous chicks look like hot babes."

Eddie responds despondently. "What's this got to do with Tim?"

"Oh yeah...that's what I was gonna say. He was wearing Tim's leather jacket, first off. But that's not all. He turned back around and started walking along the lake. So I followed him, but I kept quiet and kind of a ways behind him. 'Cause he still hadn't seen me, and I didn't fuckin' want him to."

Sensing Eddie's growing exasperation, Jill joins by his side and grabs his arm in hers, hoping to somehow sedate the thoughts now troubling his mind. As she does this Ronnie climbs over the trucks wheel well and takes her place sitting over the side of the pickup just beside Jill.

For a moment, Mike steps back and considers that the picture before him is missing his best friend, either with his arm tucked behind his girl, or standing beside his older brother subconsciously making attempts to mimic him. The thought arrests him for a few brief seconds, but he continues his monologue with no desire to invite a bleak silence.

"He started walking up to this goat trail going up the mountain. I followed him a little, but stopped not far from the base of the trail, 'cause that shit was getting steep. I could still see him though, and it was a full moon so I could make out most of everything. After so far he stopped and kneeled down and it looked like he started climbing down in the mountain, like, into a hole or a cave in the ground. I walked up closer and climbed a little until I could make it out."

Michael turns his head to face the desert no longer wishing to see the group as he had known it, only now, missing his favorite member.

"And he was climbing into some more of that tar shit. I could make it out; shit looked like it was eating him. But I swear he climbed into it. What kind of dipshit, basket case would knowingly climb into that crap? Fuckin' had to be an alien. And afterwards, I couldn't see him anymore, like he got eaten, the tar looked like it ate itself and then was gone."

"And you also don't see things like that when you're high, right?"

Ronnie jumps down from the truck and opens the back passenger door to the Catalina before sitting in the passenger seat. Mike feels as though he may have somehow impressed his disparaging consideration of their shorted group upon her, as she seems to have lost her temperate tone.

"I wasn't high. I brought some shit with me, that Blue Velvet. You remember that stuff Eddie? The good shit. I gave some to you and Tim."

Mike again grins expectantly, but meets the same vacant response from the older of the two brothers; he grows increasingly uncomfortable with the present mood of his peers.

"After that, I fuckin' hauled it out of there and just camped out further up the road from the lake near the rim. Actually, I did smoke some there, and stayed up all night freakin' out thinking that that tar shit might show up again, and fuck knows...In fact, I think I smoked the last of my bag, shit—I'm out of it then."

This thought takes hold as Mike searches through the console between the two bucket seats in his truck and finds that he had, in fact, emptied his entire bag.

"Why didn't you just go home?"

Jill asked, and knew instantly after, what the answer would be.

"Duh, I was drunk; I didn't want to be driving around on the roads in town. So I just pulled off down some dirt road and crashed in my truck."

Tossing the empty bag back into his truck, Mike slams the door shut. Instead of entering his vehicle, he plops himself into the back, driver-side seat of the Catalina.

"So where are we headed?"

He calls out through his window.

"We?" Ronnie asks with disapproval. In fact, she shares similar feelings with Mike, and finds it too disconcerting to see the man alone, when he is almost always accompanying her boyfriend. In some ways, she finds this leads to her resentment towards him.

"Shit yeah, I've got nothin' else to do. I have almost a week to kill. Plus, you know you want me to come. You wouldn't know what to do without me."

Grinning, Mike is met with Ronnie's return of a stern glare. Her facial contortions quickly melt as she considers the inkling of truth to Mike's statement. They are capable enough without him, but perhaps with him around irritating her with his off-color comments, she has something to draw her attention away from thoughts of the horrible possibilities that surround Tim's disappearance, even if his presence does somewhat remind her of Tim's absence.

Besides which, she figures, as much as she is annoyed by his relentless candor, she knows Tim could have, and has had, far worse friends than a lumbering mechanic who would go to any length to remain by his side.

"I'll just leave my pickup here. Maybe I'll get lucky and someone'll take the piece of shit. I'm tired of workin' on that damned thing."

■ 5:47PM

Mike, sharing the back seat of Eddie's car with the now irritated Ronnie, nods his head furiously, playing a non-existent guitar poorly, and singing, overwhelming the actual rendition of the song which is futilely bleating through the cars speakers.

Mike recites the memorized chorus revealing his grating, tonal-impairment.

"Mike, would you shut the hell up?!"

Eddie peers at him through the rear view mirror.

"I'm gonna blow my speakers just trying to hear the damn song. And you sound like a dying pigeon."

"Shit, you know you like these licks though."

Mike grins awkwardly and begins flicking his fingers, tearing along what must be a fairly worn and probably heavily damaged air guitar.

Eddie shakes his head smiling; "You're a dipshit, Mike."

Mike nods his head, not in agreement, but to the rhythm of the song.

"Yep." Ronnie adds and turns back to watch the stretch of dry red and yellow desert pass alongside the highway, interrupted every now and then with various species of shrubs, casual skyward stabs of saguaros, and awkward groupings of yucca trees.

Jill adds to the group's sentiment before allowing the initiation of verbal silence; "Yeah, maybe it's time to retire that thing."

"So where in the hell are we headed again? I mean, you never told me. Is it a secret or some shit?"

These questions, issued between large malicious bites into a Slim Jim, Mike offers in an additional attempt to end the silence.

"Right now we're just driving, I thought maybe we'd check out the lake and go from there, I guess."

"Wow, that's some plan Eddie! There's nothing at the lake. Remember, I was just there—"

"Do *you* remember? The strange man, with Tim's jacket climbing into a pool of tar...I think you told us about it, oh...like three minutes ago."

Jill calmly interjects, but builds sharply in sarcasm before finishing. Eddie considers this to be his wife's trademark in dialogue.

"Yeah, but like I said, he's not like there anymore, and that tar-shit disappeared too. I didn't see any more than that out there or even on the way back. I did see some of it all over the sixth, remember? They had it all blocked off."

"Nah, it's all clear now. We actually used it last night; I took Jill to Romero's before this happened. I even asked the waiter if he knew anything about it. He said that they did have it blocked off, but apparently, they got it cleared up. He said he couldn't think of how they got it done so quickly...I just remembered that—"

It comes, takes whatever it's looking for and leaves.

Why Bowling? One of the smallest towns in the west.

Why is it always out in the middle of "Podunk Nowhere" that all this weird crap happens?

And Tim—

Beginning to trail off once more, Eddie returns to the deep concentration that is usually required for the most troubling of matters. It's not entirely coincidence that the greater percentage of these times occur because of something his younger brother has or hasn't done. And thinking of this only makes Eddie miss his sibling more.

"Anyways...we might as well try the lake, so far the strangest story we've heard is yours, Mike, and the way things have been, strange is probably our best bet."

Jill stares at Eddie, still apparently lost in his own mind, and thinks as she lifts her eyebrows quirkily; *I sincerely hope he's actually watching the road and not just staring out at it.*

The car does little to comfort Jill's fears, and instead confirms her suspicion as it veers off of the stretch of highway kicking up dust along the desert floor.

"Shit!"

Returning to his senses in an instant, Eddie forces the wheel into a sharp, nearly ninety-degree rotation and returns the car to the highway. The twenty-something Pontiac doesn't typically respond well to such harsh treatment and refuses to continue, killing the engine in objection.

"Fuckin' sonofabitch!"

Eddie forces the key, but the car is steadfast in its protest and responds only with a sputter.

"What was that all about?"

Veronica removes her arms from a bracing position and slowly withdraws the shocked expression from her face.

"The car died."

This response, Eddie supplies with such a somber voice that the other passengers might have mistaken it as cool and composed, were it not for the obvious detail revealed with the accompaniment of a dazed and distant look. This is followed by Eddie violently ripping free his seat belt, throwing the driver-side door open and slamming it shut after storming out into the bleating midday heat.

Jill removes her seat belt in kind and begins to open her door. She stops as she realizes Mike has already beaten her out of the vehicle. It's just as well she thinks. Eddie, needing a mechanic and likely a place to vent would find Mike the better candidate for both applications.

"You want me to take a look at it Eddie? Sounds like the fuel filter might be bad."

Mike joins Eddie at the front of the broken down vehicle.

"Sure, go for it."

After wiping his forehead with the back of his forearm, Eddie leans on the car with arms crossed.

"You pretty rattled? Don't worry 'bout Tim. We'll find him. You'll have plenty more chances to kick his ass."

Mike slaps Eddie on the back before reaching down into the car's engine. He removes the in-line filter.

"Yeah, this things fuckin' nasty. No wonder your engines choking. You need to replace it."

"Thanks, let's just drive down to your shop and wait twelve days for the part to come."

Eddie snaps back, but quickly applies a lightened tone to his voice, after hearing the words progress.

"Or you can go fuck yourself for a second while I clean this one up a little...Dickhead!"

Mike flips Eddie the bird then taps the fuel filter on the front bumper.

"You need a rag?"

Returning to the driver door, Eddie opens it and leans into the vehicle. He raises his eyebrows to his wife and smiles to reassure her that his high spirits have not yet completely dissolved, as he reaches under his seat for a rag.

He tosses a stained red cloth to Mike, who catches it and reviews it for a second with a certain look that expresses his concern presented with trying to clean an object with a piece of fabric that isn't entirely clean itself.

Mike raises an eyebrow and frowns at Eddie.

"It'll work, just do your job, peon."

Eddie lights another cigarette and smirks.

"Alright, but you have to get me a beer when I'm done, and it better be as cold as a witch's titty."

Mike lightly cleans the filter with the worn rag. He looks up and sees that Eddie has disappeared.

"Eddie. Where the fuck did you go?"

Eddie returns with a small Jerry Can.

"Who's the peon now? Go fetch me a beer."

Michael chuckles and rinses the fuel filter with the fuel stored in the Jerry Can. He replaces it in its proper spot among the other filthy and envious engine components, and watches the engine as he dictates to Eddie;

"Start it up!"

Eddie complies and flicks the ignition then revs the car. It struggles reluctantly for a second, then starts.

Leaning out of the driver window, Eddie shouts; "You can put the gas can back in the trunk, and the red cooler has all the beer in it, but leave some for the rest of us."

Mike reveals his dexterity guzzling a beer while simultaneously taking his seat, closing the door and fastening his safety belt. After finishing three quarters of the beer in a matter of one minute, Mike repeats to Eddie; "You'll definitely need to replace that filter. I cleaned it, but it won't last long."

"Yeah, we should get right on that. Let's turn around and drive another forty miles back into town only so we can double back again."

Ronnie makes no effort to mask the cynicism of her remark.

"Wow, who stuffed a dead badger up your ass? You know, Tim told me you liked to do some weird things, but I didn't believe him."

Chuckling, Mike peels his beer label off and stuffs it inside the bottle.

"Shut up, idiot. I was joking anyways."

"Some joke, why don't you stab him too, then we can all have a big laugh."

Eddie peers at the backseats through the rearview mirror with smiling eyes, one of which winks. Shifting his attention to the highway, his eyes widen slightly as he notices a strange dark shape on the left side of the road, almost removed from view. It seems to him to be sheer luck that it should even catch his glance.

Lucky or not, that's the stuff we're looking for.

As soon as his attention is drawn to the shape, whether out of coincidence or the intent of some greater unknown party, he identifies it, or, at least, identifies it to the extent of his pre-existing knowledge of what *it* is.

"It's tempting sometimes."

Ronnie smiles looking up and notices the subtle change in Eddie's eyes.

"What do you see?" She turns around and looks out the back window of the car.

"It's that fucking tar!"

Mike yells out as if he's discovered something the others haven't.

Eddie hardly slows down as he makes a sharp U-turn on the highway and begins driving back towards the unidentified yet identifiable substance.

Jill releases her fierce grip from the door and dashboard and glares at her husband.

"I'm not sure that was necessary."

"Probably not, but if I slow down too much the car might die again. Besides, who knows how long that tar-crap will stick around."

"It makes it more exciting this way. It's like we're in this crazy high speed chase. Eddie's the last super-driving American hero of the golden west!"

Mike leans out of the window and points forward making a gun with his fingers.

"Are you drunk already?" Ronnie shakes her head.

"A little buzzed. I think I'm carrying over from last night."

"Oh Michael, whatever will we do with such a large waste of space?"

Jill shakes her head and looks to the dark substance in the quickly diminishing distance as if awaiting an answer to her rhetorical question.

Eddie slowly, not wishing to once again disturb his wife, pulls the car over beside the highway about forty feet from the black, and most certainly foreign substance. He parks the car and steps out noticing the considerable change in temperature as he leaves the cool air-conditioned vehicle. Figuring, very accurately in fact, that the heat has increased almost five degrees since last he stopped, Eddie wipes his forehead once more.

Shortly after exiting, he is joined in the sweltering heat by the rest of his company.

"So what's the plan?" Jill asks, standing by her husband and sharing his same vacant, wondering expression as they both stare into the pool of seemingly eternal darkness which stands about twenty feet before them.

"Find a stick or something." Taking his own advice, Mike begins looking for a long slim object to poke pointlessly and provocatively at the unknown material.

Ronnie, who has been silent since the party departed the vehicle, acts as if strangely mesmerized and slowly approaches the black substance.

"Ronnie, stay back. Don't get too close to that stuff."

With concern, Jill reaches out slightly as if to grab Ronnie, an impossible task considering the distance already developed between them.

Still fixated, Ronnie stands very close to the tar, uncomfortably close in Jill's mind.

"Ugh, sick man!"

Michael shouts to his friends from a short ways off.

"What is it?"

Eddie turns to see Mike hunching over with a stick, grossly fixated.

"I don't know, I think it's a dead lizard or something."

With his incredibly sophisticated investigative tool, Mike pokes the decomposing remains of what is indeed a dead lizard.

"Damnit Mike, get your ass back—"

"RONNIE!" Jill interrupts her husband with a piercing scream and lunges forward launching into a dash with her husband racing close behind her.

Without delay, Ronnie hastily creeps into the tar and in her determination lets out not a single murmur. By the time her name is ringing in the ears of anyone within a three mile radius, she is already engulfed up to her waist.

This isn't due to a poor reaction time on Jill's part, but instead could be attributed to the uncanny, otherworldly speed, with which the substance moves, coupled with Ronnie's eerie and sudden disposition of utter compliance.

"Fuck! Ronnie!"

Eddie shouts desolately and grasps Ronnie's hand, pulling with a strength only he could muster. This only remaining, visible part of her juts from a grouping of tar which now consists of an astonishingly minuscule amount, having contracted in accordance to the size of what little remains of Veronica Rawls in this world.

And almost as instantly as Eddie grabs and pulls back on Veronica's hand, with his most commendable attempt, it is harshly removed from his grip, as if pulling away in strong revulsion to the man's presence. The tar vanishes in a quick and troubling fashion and leads Eddie to wonder if it worked so quickly in a reaction to their presence, as if it only wanted one of them, and hurried its efforts to ensure no meddling could prevent its capturing and departing with the prey.

Mike reunites with the others, holding the stick by his side with a stupefied look. He drops the stick, realizing it no longer holds a purpose. Helping Eddie to his feet, the two then join Jill standing over her as she wipes the tears welling in her eyes, momentarily refusing to leave her hunched position.

ASPIRING ASCENT (WRITING ON THE WALL)

Veronica lies on her stomach sprawled out on grimy pavement nestled claustrophobically between two tall, foreboding buildings. Her position would make a passerby think she had either fallen from several stories up and is now donating her remains to the many forms of bacteria that riddle the dank alley, or had far too much to drink and is, instead, simply bedding with said bacteria for the night. A wise passerby would also note that the latter isn't a vast improvement in terms of prolonging mortality when considering these various forms of bacteria that occupy the street Ronnie currently holds in a light, full body grasp.

Ronnie slowly regains partial consciousness. She realizes she is not dead, or, at least, doesn't feel as she would expect to feel if dead. She also knows that she isn't asleep, but feels as if her body may have a difference of opinion, as she currently finds it is impossible to move.

To the extent that she can recall at current, Veronica realizes she has experienced this sensation before, a kind of sleep paralysis. She's conscious and therefore, knows she's awake, but currently can do little about it. If she could move, in any way, her eyes would be wide open and she'd be lifting herself, very quickly from the ground, which she is beginning to notice is sticky, and bears a poignant smell similar to a combination of aged popcorn butter, foot fungus, vomit, and cat urine.

"Oh God!"

She is able to vocalize her derision with the scents, but only in a slight, muted sigh muffled into the warm and harsh pavement pressing against her cheek.

As she fiercely endeavors to move, control quickly rushes back through her body. She nearly throws herself to her feet in an exaggerated, but graceful motion.

Pressing her hand against the nearby wall, she hunches over clutching her stomach and dry heaves. The promise of this act is fulfilled as Ronnie vomits, coating the lower portion of the wall with predigested, amino acid enriched stomach content. She assumes this must be the fiftieth time the wall before her has been so christened. It certainly isn't the first time and it would not likely be the last.

Ronnie's eyes scan the walls. Her hand repeatedly attests that the walls surface is not stone, adobe, concrete, or wood, as would be the case with any building in Bowling. Instead, the cold and sterile surface, as confirmed with sight, is solid metal.

The steel wall is thick in a coating of strange and visually invasive graffiti. Strange, in that it does not resemble any of the street artistry she'd ever seen between California and Arizona. Visually invasive, in that it appears to glow, intensely, in various areas as if the paint itself is not simply luminous by way of reflection or bright in contrast to the dark walls, but is somehow generating light.

It is made very clear to Ronnie; she is not in Bowling anymore, and she has no familiar with which she can share the experience, or even this realization, not even a dog.

Veronica continues to survey the several coatings of graffiti, overlapping, accompanying, and likely in some cases, responding to one another. Most of the wall paintings are very well illustrated, but impossible to understand. In those various areas that appear to be emitting a self-produced light, apparently as a means of emphasis, the paint is elevated from the surface and bears all three visual dimensions.

She finds a spot of illuminated green paint encompassing the bottom of what looks to her to be a 'Z' or possibly a number '2' and cups her face over the spot, shielding out all of the external light. The intense color radiates along her face and hands; it is nearly as bright as staring directly into a halogen light bulb. She can see through the corners of her eyes that the skin of her fingers, bathed in the green hue is made partially transparent revealing her veins, bones and tendons.

Definitely not Bowling.

This bold new world is missing a very specific scent; one she hadn't realized Bowling presented until just now. The tinge of sun-baked earth, dried grass, sycamore and tobacco is decidedly absent. This scent, to which she was apparently greatly accustomed, is replaced by a synthetic aroma composed of metal; its fatigue and decay, various burning chemical gases, heated plastics, and the smell of circuitry when it's overwhelmed and overheating. It is an improvement over the assaulting barrage she'd experienced lying on the pavement, though, some of those smells too, are still prevalent.

The sounds; faint buzzing, zipping traffic somewhere overhead, and various forms of white noise seem to assault her from every angle and at every fathomable distance. Though the vehicular noise is familiar, she realizes that in some strange way, the bustling traffic is off in its resonance.

It's wrong.

What should sound like gears, spinning wheels, brakes, and engine sounds of various pitch and depth, sounds more like winding computer fans, suction, and light speaker feedback. Ronnie is, she surmises, in a place far more active and more populated than Bowling. By a great deal, in fact, she is correct. However, she can perceive none of the subjects creating the battery of sounds, and has yet to see a single soul.

She currently stands in an empty alley somewhere on the city's floor level and has already learned one truth about the city. No self-respecting pedestrian descends to the ground level. Only vehicles can be seen flying by in the distance with such speed it is unlikely any of the passengers have any concept of the surroundings outside of their conveyance. It would seem, based on what Ronnie has noted so far, only the delinquent or desperate descend so deep into the city and infrequently so.

Hearing various forms of shouting, inane chatter, and often instructive peroration in such great abundance, she compares it to the year she spent living with her mother in San Francisco.

The crappiest time of my life.

Not necessarily due to location, but undoubtedly due to the company.

A thought which begs her to question, given the current circumstances, how long this would remain the case.

Not long enough.

While her insufferably elitist mother is certainly not present here, the atmosphere is daunting and promises very little of what Veronica desires in a town.

Laughter?

For instance.

In large enough crowds, which Veronica would wager must be swarming the streets of this city somewhere above her head, laughter would usually be present at one time or another, especially around The Quartz. It seems to Ronnie that it should be a law of nature; wherever can be found a drinking establishment, there can be found laughter, in some form, even if it is usually accompanied by drunken stupor and a trip-and-fall on the always obstinate side of the street. It occurs to her, there is no laughter here; no giggling, no chuckles, nor any joyful sound supplementing the otherwise dry conversations, and if it's wafting somewhere among all of the other vocal waveforms, it is lost, too subtle and thus rendered useless. The atmosphere, or at least, the atmosphere generated by the sound of voices, is thick with a vain apathy and monotony. Even the raised voices seem to stay within a certain range and the overall tone is far too even keel.

Again, Ronnie thinks; *nothing like The Quartz.*

The street just beyond the alley beckons Ronnie with its potential to lead her to a more sensible location and she responds walking out into the blinding light trails whizzing by in the short distance to maybe meet the noise with its transmitters. The alley stretches several hundred feet behind and before her. It is a brisk walk between the defaced and solemn walls.

As she steps out unto the incredibly thin street-side she confirms what she'd believed to be the case; no people, not even sidewalks alongside the streets. The implication, Ronnie gathers, being that citizens are not supposed to traverse to this lower level by foot. In so many new ways, Veronica is realizing the danger she is in, simply being at this ground level. Even merely standing, as is Ronnie, on the thin stretch of concrete supporting the street on her side seems to be a great risk as she can feel the wind blast generated by the thousands of vehicles bulleting by, just in front of her.

Probably not a good idea to stand here.

Stepping back, she instinctually looks down to her feet. Upon doing so, she notices that the concrete appears to be something similar to a pellucid synthetic glasswork. With large bright lights of red, green and yellow undulating in various shapes she assumes must be used for directing vehicle traffic. The lights appear to be projecting the signs and lighted directions towards the sky; she lifts her head to follow them. These large, three-dimensional projections of lighted shapes pierce, uninhibited through the structured ceiling above her and continue well beyond view. What little Ronnie can make of the holographic projections; resemble the various street-signs she is used to seeing in Bowling, only they appear to be much brighter and more refined.

In this same excessively populated sky she can also see that traffic is divided into two or more tiers; a street running just before her, adjacent to the bases of the buildings and another transparent, seeming unsubstantial, street runs alongside

planes constructed of steel and concrete shells sharing structural support with the buildings on either side of it. Beyond this
tier it is too difficult to see anything clearly, but Ronnie assumes
the streets must cross, overlap, meet and turn in multiple lay-
ers mapped not only with latitude and longitude but also an
altitude. Great numbers of additional vehicles fly past quickly,
just a few hundred feet above her, forming streams of blurring
bright lights in stretched and shapeless forms.

The conversations; those dismal, abundant and utterly un-
interesting conversations, must be billowing from somewhere
above Ronnie where the activity escalates as the city ascends
into the sky. As the transparent street is only transparent where
the vehicle traffic whips by, leaving a great amount of solid
ceiling on either side of the immediately visible street tier, it
allows more than enough space for a very busy and very large
sidewalk, where foot-traffic must progress with the same tedium shared by the conversations.

Lighted paint similar to that used on the wall in the form of
graffiti, plasters the sidewalk underside. But these vast fields
of pointless painted imagery are not graffiti; they're advertisements, thousands of demanding and occasionally persuasive
commercial pieces.

Ronnie cannot recognize any of the advertisements, but
does recognize their uses; they encompass a large gamut of
pseudo-information regarding where and what to eat and
drink, vehicles with the best performance and safety ratings
that allegedly no longer require the hassle of knowing how and
where to drive, multitudes of pharmaceuticals with products
used to treat any number of symptoms which include virtually
every sensation the human being could possibly experience at
any given time; even medications used to treat effects caused
by the use of other medications, and hundreds of images
depicting needs for members to help extend various factions,
guilds, parties, groups, associations, dogmas and institutions.

Some of the paintings are even animated and display muted forms of televised commercials. How these displays could possibly function, Veronica can only begin to imagine.

Allowing her eyes to crawl aimlessly along the ads on the ceiling they finally settle upon an animated image that does not appear to serve as an advertisement. It, instead, displays an animated information block, provided solely by an evidently self-aggrandizing company called Dotcel-Uni World Bank containing a depiction of the current weather in Domaves City, Calivadimes. Ronnie gathers; this must be the droning, blinding and generally sense-assaulting city at the bottom of which she is currently standing. Along with the current weather, temperature and location, the information block also states the barometric pressure, air-pollution, population, stock ticks, and the immediately startling time and date.

■ 8:39PM, SEPTEMBER 3RD 2176

She assumes the date and time must be accurate, as it would otherwise be a tremendously ludicrous waste of effort, money, and likely valuable advertisement real estate all to display pointlessly false information. Besides all of this, the date does seem to coincide with the surroundings in that they appear to be far more advanced than anything Ronnie can recall ever seeing before, especially in her previous diminutive, desert location.

This is all very overwhelming to Veronica and she finds herself at a rare loss for words standing in momentary awe.

A vast deal of time is spent taking in the sights and sounds before Ronnie remembers why she's there, or at least why she left Bowling. Although the prospect of having to search for Tim through a foreign land somewhere in the distant future seems disheartening to say the least, Ronnie finds herself to be excited at the idea and knows the last thing she should allow herself, would be a loss of hope.

"I guess I better get out of here, and find a way up." Ronnie says, thinking aloud, and proceeds alongside the lighted street-side flooring.

As she walks, surveying the city in hopes to find some way to reach the upper tiers, she examines the buildings; all standing tall, far beyond the second level street platforms, and in those areas where her view is not obstructed by the tiered streets she can see that most of the buildings stretch incredibly high, far beyond her field of view as if breaching the atmosphere into the expanses of space. As she walks beside the towering structures Veronica notices many share a similar, almost foreboding motif and a color scheme composed of a dark copper and a muted blue metallic hue varying only slightly from building to building. The sky-piercing monoliths vary some in terms of shape and layout, and few, even in height, as with those select stunted towers Veronica can see a vertical end.

Nothing like the buildings in Chicago or New York.

Many resemble giant cylinders with walkway tubes, streets, and rail-systems attaching them to one another and to other smaller structures suspended like islands in the sky. Others are more akin to a collection of variously sized steel boxes arranged and cobbled together into large skyscrapers in a seemingly random, but somehow fluid design.

Each building is decorated with hundreds of thousands of thin plate-glass windows adorning all sides in sometimes exceptional, but often common layouts. Exits, most of which look like minimalist slate-steel slide doors accompany these glassy features and are supported by many more signs, notifications, and advertisements. In the form of projected and animated light displays, the building signage appears to float completely unattached to its corresponding structures.

Ronnie imagines for a moment how much more drab and bleak the city might appear if it weren't blemished with the thousands of obnoxiously terse displays.

Continuing past what Ronnie counts to be the sixth mono-lithic structure of futuristic dystopian tedium, she stops and decides to attempt to enter one of the buildings.

Since Veronica can see no entrances to shops, bars, or restaurants, rather, only the various signs depicting where they could be found, she assumes the multiple levels above her must contain these destinations. Thus, after elevating to a higher level, she may find a better viewpoint with which to inspect her surroundings and find these various points of interest. It will also give her a chance to test the durability of her eyes as they will, most certainly, be assailed while taking in the sights.

She can't wait to see how grand and illustrious the insides of these buildings must be.

Ronnie recalls the number of remarks people would often make in regards the odd look of The Quartz, both positive and negative. She'd always thought it was, at least, unique and had personality, as much personality as a building could have, es-pecially in what amounts to just another roadside town. These buildings, on the other hand, appear cold and sterile with a genuinely unsettling quality of inertness.

Ronnie predicts; *White-walled insides with buttons and TV screens built into the walls everywhere, all showing random multi-colored abstract crap meant to be calming, in between commercials, of course.*

Reluctantly, Ronnie enters one of these sterile and uninvit-ing structures through a thin, semi-cylindrical metal door that connects almost seamlessly with the rounded corner of the edifice. She doesn't actually open the door, as this appears to be an unnecessary custom. Upon approaching the door, it wisps and rotates before her until, all at once, an opening is revealed. She steps into the small closet-like room which Ronnie assumes to be some sort of vestibule one must trespass before actually entering into the building's lobby. She finds herself inside a me-tallic cylinder with a brightly lit floor and ceiling, both of which glow an almost blinding white reflecting incredibly along the smooth, polished surface of the interior walls. Oddly, she notices, given the abundance of light, the interior of the cylinder is surprisingly cool, though not particularly refreshing, as the air maintains a density and essence she could only compare to that experienced inside of a commercial airliner during flight; recycled and somehow stale.

At least it doesn't smell as bad as outside.

Suddenly the section of the cylinder just in front of her, opposite the entrance, forms an animated display with a similar system, she recognizes, to that of the animated advertisements she had just witnessed projected from and upon the buildings outside. With an appearance of three-dimensions the display floats disconnected from any solid surface, reflected only slightly upon the metal surroundings. The display features several slick-looking and sharply rendered interface boxes indicating various details and specifications of the cylinder, which, according to the top label of the display, actually serves as an elevator.

A flashing section of the display indicates the floors present in the building, with Veronica's current floor ablaze and emphasized in a bright green tone. It also indicates with a depiction of a human figure similar to that seen on a bathroom door, that the current amount of occupants within the elevator is one, being her, and that she apparently weighs, although never admittedly, fifty six point seven kilograms or roughly one-hundred, twenty-five pounds, which is one-point-five percent of the maximum occupancy. The display also appears to recognize that she is female, or possibly a cross-dresser as the figure representing her wears a skirt. She can't quite fathom how any elevator would know her gender, but decides her time would not be well spent questioning such things. She feels she's likely to be presented with too many obstacles to overcome in her quest to find Tim and does not wish to be sidetracked.

Decorating various locations of the display are the, evidently standard; temperature, barometric pressure, air-pollution, population, stock ticks, short undulating news briefs, the time, date, and current weather conditions. Displayed along with these are the elevator's unique functions; a button with the word search displayed in its center, buttons to open the exterior or interior doors, a button indicating volume control beside a selectable menu that changes the soft, ambient and generally tedious elevator Muzak, and a button that enables or disables automated audio instruction or assistance. And, after some careful searching, four large buttons dominating the entire right section of the display that list the corresponding floors are found. She sticks her finger into the light depicting the second floor button which seems to bend and warp slightly as her finger pierces directly through the visual projection. A slight clicking sound is produced along with a slight electronic pulse that attempts to mimic the tactile response of button pressing. The button lights up bright yellow. She notices that the animatic featuring the elevator containing her charmingly generic female figure shows vertical movement, indicating that the elevator is travelling upwards. Otherwise, she cannot discern any change in her surroundings to indicate that this is actually the case. Being used to the clunking, equilibrium manipulating, and oft noisily grinding elevators found in her western state, she is understandably perplexed by the new experience.

Is this thing even moving?

After forming the inquiring thought, Veronica estimates a maximum of one seconds passing before the display indicates that the elevator has, in fact, arrived at floor two.

"I guess it *was*."

The lift then applies its greatest effort into drawing her attention to the operational door buttons with glowing bright lights and animated gestures begging her to press a button. She presses what she assumes to be the exterior door button, which is indicated by two triangles pointing away from one another separated by a thin vertical line. The walls, which, up to this point, were utterly seamless and limitlessly smooth, rotate quickly and reveal an opening into the crowded streets a few

feet before her. The display reminds her with a friendly lam-
bently lit animated representation that she may now evacuate
the lift as the exterior door is ajar, as requested. The walls, with
obsessive intent, become flooded with streaming arrow anima-
tions anxiously directing her to leave.

■ 8:58PM

Veronica steps out of the building's exterior, city-use elevator system and stares out onto Domaves City, tier two.
This is the city street she'd reluctantly, but reasonably imag-
ined, corresponding in sights and activity with the various noises she'd heard previously. In a word, or rather two; horrendous
and overwhelming.
"Where do I begin?"

BREAKING PACKS (DOGS OF WAR)

■ 6:42PM AUGUST 21ST 1985

Gramps, as far into the past as he can recall, has always considered himself, a 'dog' man. Although, if some oblivious fool dared to call him such a thing, he may find himself limping away with several welts and bruises cascading his torso and face. But he did in fact, love dogs, and like many of his favored dogs, hated cats, which he would, on occasion, shoot with an old air-rifle, should any of the local stray menaces try to infringe upon his land. Though he rarely likes to recall, he had once shot a dog as well, but with an actual rifle, and that being because it appeared to be rabid.

Gramps recalls the presence of two Bluetick Coonhounds and a Bloodhound plying the role of his, his brother's and his sister's best allies. Occasionally, they even served as protectors for him, his brother and sister when they were young. His father bred these Blueticks for a short period, but primarily used them, along with the Bloodhound for hunting. He often referred to the three as his "dogs of war." In a funny way, each dog had attached itself to one of the children. Gramps acquired the single Bloodhound, Mendell, as his most favored companion, one that, upon death he'd sworn to be completely irreplaceable. This stood true for many years, until Pete finally entered into his life.

At first, Gramps despised the dog, which had actually been his wife's pet, given to her as a Christmas gift from her sister, whom Gramps assumed hated him for his intrusion into the family. She did. He supported this with the belief that Pete was given to his wife Virginia, not merely as a gift, but as a despicable and hideous nuisance that would drive him to madness. This too, was true. At first, he would say he'd been defeated and that Virginia's sister, Carol, had bested him, but after a few years, the scraggly-looking, hairy creature, commonly regarded as a Picardy Shepherd, grew on him, and became another beloved member of his small, immediate family, having only surrogate children in Richard and his sons, Tim and Eddie.

The only remains of the fairly lazy, often stubborn, but usually loyal dog lay as a detached collar on the end table next to Gramps' recliner.

"Damned dog."

Gramps finds himself reclined next to the collar with the keys to his Buick in hand internally debating and struggling to decide whether he should remain in his home as he'd promised Eddie, or act upon his initial plan and leave in search of Pete, in what could possibly be the last noble effort to conclude the story of his life.

The phone rings. Gramps waits it out allowing four rings to fill the air; then answers.

"Sorry to bother you, Gramps. It's me again—"

"Hey, Eddie; I'm glad to hear from you, what's going on? Have you found Tim yet? Or Pete?"

Gramps waits expectantly for hopeful answers to all three questions.

"Actually...we've lost Veronica now."

Eddie, standing in a phone booth stares at his car through the glass door and focuses upon his wife in the passenger seat, lightly resting her face in her hand with an expression of grief and angst. He looks to the back seats and sees that Mike has found his walkman and is currently flailing his arms boisterously in an attempt to mimic apparently rapid drumming to what Eddie figures is probably Def Leppard.

Mike must have just smashed the back of Jill's seat in his careless antics, because even at the distance Eddie currently stands from the car, he can hear his wife unleashing hours of pent up fury. Eddie chuckles lightly, hoping it isn't picked up through the receiver.

Gramps takes no notice; "Shit Eddie, how the hell 'id that happen?"

"I don't know, exactly. We found some more of that black substance, and while we were all standing, I guess, just sort of, debating what to do next, or screwing around, in Mikey's case. Ronnie just jumped into the tar, and...I tried to grab her but, just like that, she was gone. And we can't find any more traces of that black crap...or Tim, or Ronnie. God only knows what the hell's happened to 'em all."

"Eddie, you'll find Tim, and you'll find Ronnie when you do. Whatever's goin' on, wherever they're goin' they've all been takin' to the same place. I'm sure of it. And I've been thinkin' I'm gonna break my promise and go out and find Pete with you. It's been too many damn years of things happening with me just sitting here waiting for my time to come."

"Gramps, I don't—"

"No Eddie, you ain't talkin' me out of this. Damnit I'm gonna die soon anyways. I'm so old it doesn't even bother me thinkin' 'bout it. So what've I got to lose?"

Gramps throws the lever controlling the recliner forward and returns to a sitting position.

"What gets to me is when I'm thinkin' I'll die just sittin' here and they find me slumped in my sleep with an empty bottle and a dog collar in my hand. That's not gonna happen. And Eddie, if you don't turn the hell around and come pick up my old ass, I'm goin' out on my own. I'll get Pete back and figure all this out, or I'll die tryin' to get somethin' done!"

Gramps spurted out his words in near shouts insistent that they not fall on deaf ears.

With this sincere performance having served its purpose, Eddie responds; "Gramps, we're at least a hundred miles out of town. I'll tell you what. We're going to shoot south to Wilbanks. If you head out now, it'll be about an hour's drive or so from you, and about the same for us, so we can meet up there...you ever been to the Red Cliff Café?"

"A few times. Shit coffee, but they've got good rhubarb pie. You wanna meet up there?"

"Yeah, I think that'll be alright. It's mostly just a straight shot along the highway. We'll meet up there, have dinner...and *pie*. And maybe find a motel in town."

Eddie is certainly uneasy with the thought of having the old man drive an hour alone with the sun already setting, but trusts that Gramps will live up to his promise of embarking on a search all his own; a far less appealing idea.

"I'll be fine Eddie. You and I know I used to drive trucks in the war. I've driven through a lot worse than some dusty old desert. And I can still see shapes out my one good eye."

Gramps cackles.

"That's not funny Gramps. You drive safe, and I'll see you soon. Until then, Gramps."

"I'll be there Eddie. Bye."

Displaying their similar tendencies in phone conversations, with the last few words from each becoming distant as the phone prepares to dispatch, Eddie and Gramps return their handsets to their respective bases almost simultaneously. With less than a nanosecond between hang-ups, the execution couldn't have been performed better had it been intentional. This remarkable occurrence is made even more unusual when accounting that this is always the case with every telephone conversation between the two. With this particular occasion being the most perfectly timed, it is almost as if the situation itself is trying to protest its own significance, being that it would be the last conversation the two ever share with one another.

Gramps enters his garage and flips the lights on, only to find his vehicle absent. In place of the usual oil stains on the cement block that would typically appear below his now invisible Buick, is the tar. The viscous, obscure, and relentless interloper which had quickly become the bane of his existence compounding the absolute of his most recent losses, has now enveloped and removed the car from his garage.

"You Goddamn no-good pile of shit!"

Stomping his rage into the ground Gramps spits the words out from his blisteringly heated face.

Without hesitation the aging widower proceeds with a new course of action. Walking forward in a very determined, though sluggish pace, Gramps steps into the black matter, and breaks his agreement to rendezvous with Eddie. Once the substance reacts, doing so with a quick and terrible aggression, Gramps stops and stiffens, knowing he is incapable of accomplishing much in his resistance. He instead, allows the materials to devour him and though he makes no movement to fight back, the tar responds viciously and fiercely as it claws and scrabbles along his body forcing him down as if declaring its dominance and enforcing the old man's submission without regard to his acceptance.

■ 7:56PM

Rhubarb is often debated as to whether it is a vegetable or a fruit, appearing to cultivate in a manner more similar to a carrot or beet, yet due to its taste is often used as a fruit. In either case, with Eddie and the group he's accompanied to the café, it is regarded to be disgusting in any of its uses. In a pie, it is very tart and requires a vast amount of sugar to disguise the intensity of its natural taste.

And sure enough, with the remnants of the spring atrocities still lingering into the summer, Eddie notes the café does feature it, on its poorly scrawled pie board, with a claim to its being the best in the state. A declaration Eddie has no desire to trial.

"Guess Gramps ain't here yet."

Mike states, expecting this announcement to be novel, as if the group hadn't yet noticed this most obvious fact, given that the restaurant's current occupancy consist of themselves, a couple in a booth, a waitress, busboy, and the cook.

"Ya don't say."

Jill ensures that Mike realizes the obviousness of his statement with her favored snarky response.

"Let's just go ahead and get a table."

Eddie finds a seat at the first booth from the entrance.

The waitress takes their drink orders, which include two iced teas, one with two lemons, and a tall glass of MGD on tap, which Mike considers to be a feature that can either make or break a restaurant.

Eddie knows that the lead-footed Gramps, with his house on the side of town nearest the exit to Wilbanks, should likely have beaten them to the restaurant by several minutes and begins to grow concerned with his absence. With the advent of such recent, strange events and the resulting increase in the amount of missing persons, any delay becomes cause for concern.

Mike notes Eddies disposition and lightly slams the table adding laughingly; "It's Miller Time!"

"Shut the hell up Mike," is Eddie's reply.

"Bonehead," is Jill's.

But, for a moment at least, Mike is successful in shifting Eddie's attention, so he continues with his objective.

"I actually stopped here to use the toilet once. I wrote on the stall—I'm trying to remember how it went."

The two watch Michael furrow his brow, scratch his chin, and look away into the distance in response to a great search now taking place within his mind.

"Oh yeah, now I remember…Here I am, on this commode, dropping another giant load. I wipe my ass, but get my hand, so I wipe it on the towel stand.'"

"That's very nice. And sadly, is probably the cleverest thing you've ever come up with."

Jill patronizes, but isn't successful in masking her need to smirk at Mike's remarks.

"How the hell do you get it on your hand?"

Eddie, however, openly chuckles at his friends remarks.

"Like, when you wipe and the toilet paper tears and the shit gets on your hand. It happens to everybody."

Mike adds this last sentiment with an apparent need for reassurance.

Addressing, Jill no longer masks her laughter; "I can honestly say that has never happened to me."

The drinks arrive, but the three continue to delay in placing their meal order. Mike pauses and appears to be in deep thought once again; he finally returns to the couple with a statement reflecting what's really on their minds; what they've been trying to avoid.

"He's not gonna show up, is he?"

Eddie shakes his head.

"Nope, I don't think we'll be seeing Gramps." He follows this statement by standing up and retreating to use the restaurant's phone.

"What the fuck is going on with shit, man?"

Mike finally allows himself to become visibly upset.

"It's alright. We don't know for sure that anything's happened. He could just be late."

Jill tries to be reassuring, but has considerable doubt, which reveals itself with ease in well-defined stress lines on her face.

I NEVER WANTED TO GO (TO SPACE)

■ SOME DATE AND SOME TIME

The only kid I knew who went to space camp, I beat his ass and took his Duncan Yo-Yo.

Though the attack was unrelated to the boy's choice of summertime activities, and more the result of resentment due to the boys haughty, braggart tendencies, Tim was of a lesser privileged family in comparison to the son of a judge. Tim can recall, however, using the space motif in his verbal assault while committing diverse forms of battery. Tim had decided that day, if the class of people who would one day travel through space should resemble his childhood victim in any way, then he would never have the desire to leave the planet.

Maybe Eddie did, when we were kids, he had those posters of Saturn and Buck Rogers and shit.

Tim recalls ripping up the Buck Rogers poster after Eddie poured water over his "Moto-Rev" G.I. Joe Jeep. The Jeep still worked once it had been allowed to dry, but Eddie never replaced that poster. So Tim, using all of his crayons and at least four dedicated hours, drew a replacement Buck Rodgers poster for Eddie's ninth birthday.

Tearing up some, Tim quickly decides to stray from the thought of his brother, as it currently only serves to depress him.

He returns to his original train-of-thought and figures that it must be elsewhere; elsewhere from Earth, where he finds himself reunited with his small friend. If it is Earth, he assumes, something severely devastating has occurred.

"What do you think? Is this Earth? Or Mars, or something... Nogales maybe?" Tim tilts his head down peering past his left shoulder and finds Pete staring back up at him with a quizzical look.

Pete proposes that it is entirely likely they no longer find themselves navigating the surface of the Earth; the current atmospheric pressure presents a very discernible difference from any known Earthly domain. This, coupled with the curiously prevalent scent of ammonia among two other unidentifiable gases Pete is able to extrapolate from the air, leads him to believe their whereabouts to be somewhere far from their own planet and likely vast stretches beyond their galaxy. He continues to ponder these thoughts as he returns his glance to the off-putting horizon.

Tim concludes the admittedly one-sided conversation; "Exactly Pete...who the fuck knows."

Finding the potentially toxic levels of gas in the air to be very unsettling Pete wonders if his companion is able to detect them and draw his same suppositions. In an attempt to bring these alarming thoughts to Tim's attention, Pete lets out several hurried distress calls and wags his tail tumultuously as they continue walking.

"Damnit Pete, shut the hell up! I'm getting another fuckin' headache...Smells like piss, big time." At least, it appears, the olfactory detection does not elude him.

Pete whimpers and abandons his attempts to alert the man, who clearly lacks the ability to comprehend the possible toxicity of the atmosphere.

Several hundred feet pass in silence as they continue in no particular direction leading to no particular destination. To the extent that either party can derive from the landscape, there is no sign of civilization to be found for miles traveling any direction. Therefore, no direction could necessarily be a poor choice, nor could it be a strong one. Continuing aimlessly, with an absolute lack of decisive options appears to be the way of the world upon which they currently find themselves standing.

"Eugh! This shit makes me sick." Tim inhales and collects the mucus building within his nasal tracts in one grating snort and hocks the amalgam into the air at his right side.

He then inserts another cigarette between his lips, lights it, draws it in and exhales; "That's better. Get that piss taste out of my mouth."

Pete considers their predicament, and estimates that given their current rate of travel and their energy exertion as consequence, in addition to their semi-toxic surroundings and their lack of sustenance, they should likely die within three hours. He likely being first and Tim following shortly thereafter. They're only hope would be to find an isolated enclosure with a more hospitable atmosphere which contains both food and water. He places the probability of this advantageous outcome in a very low percentage, roughly two-point-five.

Tim, having gained five feet beyond Pete in the past two minutes, trips and rolls down the side of a tall, but fortunately not very steep, cliff. He quickly shoves out his arms and in several clumsy, hurried moves, managing to climb back to his feet, dust off his jacket and jeans, then regain what little composure he has been allowed to maintain. He looks backwards, staring up at Pete, standing at the edge of the cliff. Pete is not looking down upon Tim, as Tim had assumed would be the case. Instead, he seems to be peering very intently just beyond Tim, as if something incredibly significant has caught his eye. Tim turns his head and follows Pete's line of sight.

Not far beyond the base of the cliff, there appears to be a small enclosure. Floating unattached to either the building or the ground just beside the structure, a strikingly large, orange, glowing sign dwarfs the actual building and displays its function in several completely foreign characters, generating foreign words. One of the flashing images displayed on the sign resembles a fuel pump crossed with a giant sparkplug. And at the very bottom are a few red and yellow icons and characters which flash continuously designating some kind of warning or perhaps cautionary advisement. Tim's first thought when rendering an assumed close-up version of the building in his mind, is gas station. The absurdity of the thought of a gas station in the middle of nowhere, on some unknown planet, in God knows when, is not lost on Tim.

He laughs, almost deliriously so.

Pete forgives this, as he too feels the heightened state of bliss accompanying the incredibly unlikely sight. The thought that they might have found some form of civilization, some form of survival, or at the very least, some form of bearing in this barren landscape is almost overwhelming.

Tim progresses quickly, but with caution, down the sloping cliff and is soon followed closely by the hurried jogging of a clearly excited Pete.

Once at the base, they both break into a full-speed pursuit towards the as-of-yet unidentifiable development. As they quickly advance, the large orange-lit sign appears to reduce in size when compared to the building but seems to maintain the same overall size, perspective and position in terms of the running pair's points of view, as if the sign were a projection emitted just beyond their eyesight attached somehow to their individual heads. Clearly, an optical illusion, but neither Tim, nor Pete can fathom how it is achieved. Once within four dozen feet of the edifice, Tim stops abruptly with Pete following suit.

The unusual establishment resembles a long, steel, grey and light green cylinder stretched horizontally and halved by the planet's surface fading lightly from sight into the shifting fog. The front of the building features a large, darkly hued door illuminated with several white, orange and red lighted displays revealing several sleek lines and more unfamiliar characters neatly arranged around the doors circumference and horizontal center.

One sizeable, brightly flashing and semi-transparent display section located near the center of the door floats untethered in a similar fashion to the large sign above the structure. Just beyond this flashing exhibit of lights is what appears to be the remarkably petite seam of the door, running unabated from the ground to the ceiling.

From one side of the cylindrical structure, several wide tubes protrude and reach down into the planet's surface like catheters draining or pumping either out of or into the peculiar structure.

On the opposite side of the cylinder, similar tubes travel into another structure which looks to Tim like some kind of giant cubed engine with five large pistons rotating and pumping ferociously while producing an apparently electrically charged, blue liquid byproduct that travels through a single transparent hose behind the pumping machine and into a small chamber nestled into the side of the main cylinder.

Tim cannot begin to fathom what purposes any of these alien constructions could serve, but continues to be reminded of the gas stations that mark nearly every hundred feet of the United States. This is likely because located on the cylinder's side opposite that of the pump machine is a station-like canopy perched atop three centered steel support beams, hovering over several of the sparkplug/fuel pumps similar to the graphic depicted on the sign.

"Damn...what a trip."

Tim's words, although issued quietly, do not go unnoticed.

The orange sign depicting the purpose of the establishment begins flashing several thousands of scrambling squares and quickly reform into words Tim can actually understand. In plain, everyday American English the sign states with great pride taken in its ability to translate:

Hello,
| Kind sir and unidentified accomplice |

Welcome to:

Prictex Premium^ebr
Energy and Travel Service Center

Now offering High-Grade Prictex-C Charges!
Available at any of our 4,363 Edirthaimes locations

**WARNING | EXPIRED SERVICE CENTER 334 | DUE FOR
DESTRUCTION: 09:15 :: 02:28:3147
We're terribly sorry for this inconvenience.**

Please retreat to the recommended distance of ~300 feet until 25
days, 14 hours, and 16 minutes have past.

18:59 :: 02:03:3147

Please refer to your yPrict to find another of
our 4,363 fully-operational service centers.

Failure to comply invites enforcement

In addition to the now legible sign, a voice is emitted from somewhere within the station; *"Greetings, unknown traveler, though we always value your patronage and wish to implore your continued use of Prick-techs Premium Service Centers, now offering High-Grade Prick-techs-C Charges at unbeatable rates, please disperse immediately. This center, center three-thirty-four, is now defunct, but rest assured, with the four-thousand, three-hundred and sixty-three fully-operational centers located in Ee-dur-thame, you need only hop, skip, or jump to find the ever-dropping rates and highest quality energy only available at Prick-techs Premium Service Centers. Please refer to your 'ee-pricked' for service center locations and details. Failure to comply invites enforcement."*

Though Pete could not read the sign in either of the translations it provided, and though he could not quite understand the strangely delighted voice that stated the commercially oriented warning and disturbingly saccharine threat, in his still short life, he's seen plenty of flashing red lights and the typical human reactions to said lights and, as such, he knows the next desired course of action. Being an often loyal and usually obedient canine, Pete would likely have no issues in following Tim and whatever choices he makes.

Tim, with his ability to read and understand the language presented vocally and visually, agrees with Pete in his translation of the flashing lights as a not-so-friendly warning and strong suggestion to leave very soon

However, at this moment, Pete's mind, interrupted, is now strictly focused on a strikingly familiar smell.

It's him.

I know it's him.

He must have been here. Norman, you old fool, why didn't you stay put, continue on with your life and await my return, or even accept my absence. Surely, my loss would ease with time. Why did you have to follow us to this poisonous place? And furthermore, how did you follow us here?

You were here, after all...the scent is so faint. Could so much time have passed since you were here? Maybe the atmosphere is obscuring your smell.

Pete inches forward some, unnoticed by Tim, still staring at the large, foreboding sign and scratching his head at the meaning of the numbers that should signify an upcoming date, followed by the remaining time and the current date, which if he's reading accurately, are all very perplexing.

The smell is stronger here.

Pete concludes and for a brief moment searches the area to fine tune the olfactory hot point. His powerful nose performs well and points him towards the cylinder flexing nostrils to both emphasize the smell and display the triumph of discovery.

It seems to be emanating from the cylindrical station base. It's unlikely, but the old man may still be there. The off-chance is enough to warrant investigation, if he is present, then he will need our help, and possibly we, his. If not, then perhaps he will have left behind some indication as to where he has proceeded.

"So much for that idea. We should probably get outta here. That thing basically said it was gonna call the cops...or whatever passes for cops around here."

Tim turns his sight down, away from the disappointingly insidious sign, and looks for an agreeable response from the dog. As he does, however, Pete bursts into a quick sprint towards the large entrance to the cylinder.

"Godamnit Pete! Don't run off. It's dangerous here...I think."

Tim enters into a chase after Pete, but finds that he is no match for the unbelievably swift dog.

After a short minute, or a minute that seems to pass quicker than most for Tim, as he rarely finds himself in high-speed chases after dogs barreling along downward sloping terrain, Tim manages to catch up with the suddenly stationary Pete. Frantically clawing away at the access to the cylinder, Pete makes several admirable attempts to leap towards the display panel in hopes of discovering the method of its use, and thus, assumingly, the operation of the door. He doesn't manage to make any such discoveries and instead resorts to producing an excited and continuous barking.

"What the hell, Pete? If this is how you always act, I'm surprised Gramps missed you—Fuck, I gotta stop smoking."

Tim places his hand on the door and leans over in an attempt to steady his breathing and slow his heart rate. He shakes his head and smiles at the dog, now staring at him precociously while wagging his tail. Pete has succeeded in encouraging his desired outcome.

"Somethin's definitely got you excited, dog. So, what's in here? You smell food?" Tim confusedly begins to investigate the door and accompanying display panel, only to reach the conclusion;

"I have no idea how to open this shit."

He kicks the bottom of the door lightly and stares for some seconds at the display. The entrance display has apparently received the same translation as the sign, as it reads, in words clear enough to Tim;

'Prictex Premium[ebr], Energy and Travel Service Center, now offering High-Grade Prictex-C Charges, is closed; this center has been declared defunct and is due for destruction in twenty-five days, fourteen hours, and sixteen minutes. Please disperse immediately and thank you for your valued patronage. Failure to comply invites enforcement.'

"Fine, invite enforcement, maybe they can tell us what the hell's going on."

Pete whimpers. Tim's attempt to communicate verbally with the door implies his lack of ideas regarding how to proceed. Pete worries; *I sincerely hope this is not his only course of action.*

Below the advertisement interspersed with dire warnings is a large, rounded rectangle with the words; 'PUSH TO ENTER' in its center. It appears to be inactive as it is very lightly displayed in a grey hue. Nevertheless, Tim pushes his finger into the ghostly floating button. His index finger proceeds just through the panel causing a slight distortion in the display and a tangible sensation, but appears to have no other effect.

"Worth a shot, I guess. Come on Pete, we're not getting in there."

Tim reaches down and attempts to grab Pete who resists and lets out a short, low-toned growl, much to Tim's surprise.

"What is it with you? You dumbass dog."

Tim considers for a moment his few options; he could guiltily leave the dog behind, likely being far more lost without the companion he's actually grown to appreciate, he could try to persuade the impossibly stubborn mutt to come with him and probably be burdened with having to keep after him every time he inevitably attempts to take off and return to the station, or he could try, again, to find some way into the strange structure seizing Pete's curiosity and admittedly, his own.

Tim places his head and ear unto the door and peers sideways looking directly at the strange round protuberance which holds the lens emitting the panel's display. At first glance, he does not notice any seams or holes, or any other such blemishes that would indicate some way of opening the aperture. However, as he focuses he discovers, very close to the door's surface on the right side of the displays lens panel, a thin, dark and barely visible rectangular indentation. Pulling his head back he wraps his hands around the panel and digs his right index fingernail into the indentation. He jerks several times and only manages to lose his gripping on the slick metallic surface.

A simple idea then sparks within the otherwise bewildered mind of Timmothy Chapel. He retrieves his obviously scrapped Sony Walkman radio, pulls out the antenna and snaps it off over his leg. He'd considered using the Regency, but figured since it, at least, was making an attempt to serve some purpose; he would spare it from destruction, for the time being. He surveys the reddened ground around him and finds a small rock which he then uses to hammer the tip of the broken antennae into a thin rectangular end using the solid metal door as a stable base for this incredibly precise and complicated procedure. Once satisfied, Tim jams the antenna tip into the indentation and proceeds to hammer it in deeper into the rectangular crevice with the rock.

Cranking on the antenna while trying to dislodge the panel appears to be fruitless; Tim responds by hammering the antennae once more. This time, the antenna creeps deeper into the panel, making several cracking sounds. Following this, the display shudders distorts and disappears.

The door does not open.

Tim realizes he shouldn't have assumed it would, and that he likely only succeeded in making matters worse. Even so, he takes one last long swing with the rock clutched tightly in his palm and strikes directly into the antenna, which snaps off at the end after sliding another few forcefully acquired inches into the panel. The panel then snaps a few more times and a short seep of black smoke emanates around the lens signifying a shortage, probably the second or third.

Wrapping his hands around the remaining antenna nub, Tim yanks back, without any real idea of what his intentions could be at this point. But as he does this, the metal casing around the lens comes loose and he manages to pull it off.

Excited with his success in a possibly meaningless endeavor, he smiles down at Pete.

Pete whimpers once more. *He just destroyed the panel which served as our only means of decrypting the locking mechanism of the door...and he takes pride in this.*

Tim returns his attention to the now ruined remains of digital projection technology. What Tim discovers, is the most confusing array of the smallest circuitry, wires, and fuses he has ever seen. He also notes, that the indentation currently being violated by a broken antenna is actually some kind of port which was once wired safely into the circuitry. Knowing that he is clearly in uncharted waters, Tim decides to continue with his destructive endeavor and smashes the largest chip he can find, located just beside the port.

Please no more. Pete whimpers and barks in an effort to vocalize his plea.

Unknown to Tim, and Pete, the XenctMX-032 model doors, used in all Prictex Premium[ebr] stations are very popular among many companies because of their markedly low manufacturing cost. The trade-off for this being, of course, they are also notably lacking in secure design, and are by no means impenetrable. They are designed instead to trigger a Prictex[ebr] proprietary alert system which signals the Prictex[ebr] Corporation of intrusions and activates an interior system designed to introduce an oneirogenic gas to the buildings and its inhabitants, forcing them into unconsciousness until they are retrieved by Prictex[ebr] employed security officers. This security system is very effective when in use, however, fortunately for Tim, as this particular station is deemed defunct, it was decided to be cost-effective to remove, and likely reuse, the security system leaving the poorly secured door as the only means of deterrence.

Also unknown to Tim, and Pete, the emergency entry   detection and processing unit for the XenctMX-032 model doors is located just beside the yPrict-Direct port and is designed to be considerably larger, and therefore, more noticeable than any of the other chips and circuits. When the unit is shut-off properly via the direct port, or, in this case improperly, by being obliterated, the door responds by letting out a short squeal and giving into the employees or, in this latter instance, intruder's demand, by opening. The E-E – D-P-U, or Ee-dep-pew as it is often referred, is designed to be the most noticeable unit in the door's system as to draw any intruder's attention, being that it is the cheapest to manufacture and most easily replaceable unit. The doors corresponding opening action is activated because the only foreseeable reason for someone wishing to destroy any portion of any door, would be in an attempt to open or bypass it, and thus giving into the intruder's desire prevents any further damage being caused. As with all products manufactured at this time, self-preservation implying cost-effectiveness, is desirable. The squeal indicates that the E-E – D-P-U has been activated; or compromised and that if it is not followed by the doors opening, *it is instructed to employees that they need to report what is surely a malfunction.*

The door opens.

The improbable duo enter the room simultaneously sharing an easy and cautious pace. Tim is immediately made aware of the incredible luminescence of the interior lighting as it caresses every surface, every nook, and every cranny with a white glow. The benefit of this being that no detail within the structure is hidden. However, as the room appears to have been all but ransacked, it illuminates and reveals little that at first glance sparks Tim's interest. He begins to wonder why he'd just spent time and effort breaking and entering into a building that has been so thoroughly picked clean, and for that matter, why the security system even bothered defending an evidently empty room.

The door, which had previously been assaulted by invaders and responded by giving into their demands, assumes, as the invaders have yet to make any effort to leave, it would be safe to close without causing offense and risking further energy expenditure. As it does, a brief moan echoes within the largely vacated room and signifies the activation of the air filtration unit which quickly proceeds to dissipate any lingering levels of gases deemed toxic and replaces them with the filtered remains of a familiar combination of oxygen, nitrogen, argon and any particles picked up and recycled from previous visitors. Tim is not able to identify the exact elemental reconstruction of the air, but does note the disappearance of the tinge of ammonia.

After a few deep breaths Tim exhales;

"Finally, some fresh air, or at least better air. Now instead of piss it smells like a convenience store."

Pete tags along as Tim takes a brief surveilling walk through the interior, and notices that the size is less than half that which he'd estimated only moments before entering. He supposes this isn't uncommon, as much of the building would be used for stocking goods and service machinery, but even so, the interior is unusually cramped in comparison to the exterior of the building.

Tim, being used to stations which contain a collection of shelves and refrigerated units containing food, beverages, car products, cigarettes and the occasional magazine rack, also notes the odd size and complete lack of shelving as he finishes his brief preliminary stroll.

The station contains a couple of tipped over table sets, some decrepit benches and a shielded, sleek metallic recess in the corner of the room which bears another of the panels projecting the detached display. Like the previous projections, the display beckons Tim's attention.

Approaching the display, the alcove surrounds Tim with a bright luminescence as it initializes a calming blue and orange lighting scheme matching the accompanied display, which too becomes more illuminated in response to his proximity. In a graphic depiction, he can now clearly read, it states:

Welcome to Prictex Premium[ebr]
Energy and Travel Service Center

Please choose one of the following:
| Start Shopping |———————| Order Fuel(s) |
| Check Prictex Account |———————| Speak to An Associate |
| REQUEST EMERGENCY ASSISTANCE |

21:01 :: 02:03:3147

He presses his finger through the *'start shopping'* button and is again mesmerized by the responding lighted graphics of the holographic display. A verbal response is revealed after a short animated transition;

We're sorry, we seem to have encountered an error; ERROR CODE 691: Access denied, this service center is no longer operational. Please speak to an associate or request emergency assistance.

Accompanying this text is another very small line located at the bottom of the display reading;

Prictex Premium^ebr Service Center Associates
Level 5 *please*
| log in here |
or connect a
Prictex Premium^ebr Service Center Level 5 authorized yPrict.

With his finger hanging over the area stating *'log in here'* Tim assumes that as its design corresponds with the others which had proven themselves to be interactive; it, too, must be. He presses the *'log-in here'* block.

It *is* a button and it *is* functioning.

The display then changes to reveal another screen which requests Tim's 'Level Five' login credentials. With the words at the top stating; *'Level Five security clearance login credentials.'* Tim thinks there would be some complex and intricate system of identification process involved, but to his surprise, the screen simply requests a username, and a password. Though he has no idea what either of these could possibly be, he considers that something so simple as providing two words could hardly be very secure. With this in mind, he presses username, and the display issues a secondary tier which protrudes in front of the first display. This secondary screen features what looks to Tim to be a very futuristic computer keyboard, only it contains several additional icons he can't identify. Deciding to stick with the keys he can identify, Tim presses them slowly and spells; *'username'* followed by the pressing of the return key. He then repeats the process for the password, using the word; *'password'*.

The secondary tier disappears leaving the first screen which displays the flashing words; *'One moment. Processing...'* This screen is quickly replaced with another stating; *'login authentication failed, please try again.'*

Tim is then returned to the original login screen. He tries several other failed combinations with no intention of ever succeeding in anything other than the pointless passing of time. However, the very last combination he tries, which is a random pressing of various letters followed by a sequence of numbers; *'Username: assffe dfgghui; Password: 123456,'* yields a successful result as Tim is directed to a screen titled;

'Prictex Premium^ebr Service Center Level 5 Associate Operations'.

Assffe Dfgghui, a native of the planet Austmophine, moved to the neighboring planet, Edirthaimes, with his parents, late in the summer of 3138. His father had received a foreman position in a large Maeloid mining operation about thirty minutes east of the service center Tim currently finds himself raiding. Having made a successful jump into a more prosperous life, Mr. Dfgghui decided that his son should also adopt greater aspirations, and rather than wasting hours at home playing games in his personal virtual simulation chamber, occasionally leaving only to venture out with his similarly ambition-impaired friends to game in virtual simulation cafes, he should make the effort to become a contributing member of society, and get a job.

Assffe hated the idea but knew his father would not let up, so he accepted defeat and applied at the local Service Center and was given a base level, level 5 position, as an inventory managing associate, where his primary duty was ensuring the computer which managed the inventory was functional and accurate using various algorithms to routinely check its inventory database. He cared little about the job, and spent most of the day playing games on his yPrict.

Tim is not aware of any of this, but when the employee identification image appears in the top-left corner of the display, depicting the pale, ghostly white-skinned, blue-haired, black and beady-eyed alien teenager, Assffe, with the most apathetic and contemptible look Tim has ever seen, he begins to suspect as much.

"What the hell is that? What a little freak."

Tim finds himself berating the image to Pete, who, though looking up, conveys no interest in Tim's opinion of the disillusioned teenager's employee photo.

"Gooney-looking motherfucker."

Tim adds, just in case.

He, at least, likely understood how to open the door, proposes Pete, internally.

Tim returns his attention to the useful portion of the screen, which follows:

Prictex Premium^ebr Service Center Level 5
Associate Operations

Hello Inventory Management Associate; Assffe Dfgghui

Please choose one of the following:
| Quick Check inventory |————————| Access Inventory Warehouse |
| Employment Information |————————| Contact Supervisor |
| REQUEST EMERGENCY ASSISTANCE |

21:23 :: 02:03:3147

Tim does not find any of the options to be particularly useful save for the button he decides to press; '*Access Inventory*

Warehouse'. He assumes the corresponding result would be another screen displaying several more useless options he can exhaust until he grows completely jaded with the entire affair.

Tim, as he is realizing to be the case far too often, is wrong.

Instead, the screen disappears completely and the corner alcove becomes a blank reflective white. The wall beside the corner panel bay slides down in a single, rapid movement revealing the large inventory warehouse that encompasses the remainder of the unused building.

The warehouse is considerably darker than the area Tim perceives to be the station's convenience store. Instead of the overwhelming lighting system that seems to emit from unseen areas in the ceiling and walls, the warehouse appears to be illuminated with the natural light created by the exterior and the planet's bright orange star. The side walls of the warehouse appear invisible until they reach an eight foot height where they gradually become visible, curving into a completely opaque and rounded ceiling. It almost appears as if the ceiling were suspended in midair eight feet above the ground with its opacity bleeding into the outside sky. Tim knew this couldn't be the case, as he'd seen the outside of the building, and there are certainly walls present, unless they'd somehow dissolved after he'd entered the building. The back wall is also completely invisible and meets abruptly with the sharp edge of the ceiling. Finding the seeming impossibility of the structure to be eerie, if not entirely perplexing, Tim turns around with the intention to leave. Unfortunately, he no longer finds the store which was once present behind him seconds before.

Instead, the door which opened from the store and into the warehouse has been replaced with an open view of the outer terrain just beyond the building. He can even see the hill he and Pete recently raced down. In disbelief he continues forward, not entirely sure of his expectations. Before he reaches the outside, the scene before him crawls up and reveals beneath it the store he'd just departed. It becomes apparent, though still confusing; it is the door depicting the outer scene much like the walls surrounding him.

Tim looks down at the dog sitting just beside him expressing a look of absolute bewilderment; he is met with a similar look from Pete which seems to say;

'How could these insane optical illusions be of any use to someone working inside an inventory warehouse?'

Suddenly the thought is stripped from Pete's mind as he is reminded why he was so eager to enter the accursed building. The smell of the old man wafts from the back corner of the warehouse and he responds with a quick dash to find it.

"What the hell dog? Did you just remember what we came in here for?"

Tim follows his companion at a much slower pace and looks around at the various shelving systems, storage tubes, compartments, and crates. All are completely vacant, and all with display panels depicting products that should be stored within, but are decidedly absent.

"Assffe's been slacking on the job...stupid freak."

Tim finds his own comment amusing and chuckles briefly before turning his gaze to Pete, who is jumping erratically in front of what looks like a heavy duty storage locker, with yet another of the Prictex[ebr] system displays.

The display stuns Tim as he reads through it. Though it is another associate operations screen, it lists operations for a level 3 associate, a supervisor by the name of Norman Donaldson. The name is not what shocks Tim, however, as he does not recognize it. What does hit him like a massive brick to the face, is the image in the top left corner of the screen.

"It's Gramps."

LIFE WAS EASY (WHEN IT WAS BORING)

It couldn't stay easy forever. Eddie knew this. He also knew that, at least in his life, the instant things becomes too routine something drastic is surely to occur; more often sooner than later. These chaotic shifts forcing new effects into Eddie's life are very typically found to be in direct relation to something Tim has caused. Though, this is not entirely intentional; all of Tim's life, or at least the majority of which Eddie is aware, Tim has had the unfortunate habit of being in the wrong place at the wrong time. Eddie supposes his greatest issue with Tim is his reluctance to actually deal, independently, with these situations of inauspiciousness. Instead, he always seems more apt to allow others to overcome his various obstacles; a task Eddie finds most commonly falling into his hands.

But even with all of the past trouble Tim has seen, Eddie grasps the foreboding realization that this is the worst. Eddie hopes that whatever has happened to Tim, he abandons his typical reliance on his older brother; as though Eddie is determined, his doubts are quickly growing.

Jill takes notice of Eddie's draining confidence expressed through his corresponding increase in subdued behavior. They both rose from slumber in the small two-star motel room early, at around six-o-clock, and the entirety of their conversations in the nearly three hours since this awakening consisted of *'Good morning'* and *'I'll make some coffee'*. During this time she, too, remained very silent, as she had been collecting and evaluating conversation possibilities within her head. With this process, she applies great internal efforts in determining the best possible approach to help alleviate her husband's troubled mind.

She decides to initiate with this dialogue;

"When I was nine I lost my cat, and I remember my mom telling me *'the most important thing when you lose something you love, is not to become lost with it'* or something like that. I don't remember exactly what she said, but it made me feel better, not really because of what she said, I don't know if I really understood it...I mean, I was sad I lost the cat, but after about a week I'd already figured I wasn't going to see her again."

Looking to Eddie, Jill finds that he is listening, but only with a strained interest, especially as he is not entirely certain of her intended take-away from the conversation. He is only hoping she concludes with a summary he can fully understand.

"When she said that, I was mostly upset because I was thinking they thought it was my fault and they'd never let me have another cat, so when she said that, I was relieved because I figured it meant she didn't blame me. And like a month later I got another cat."

Jill pauses again and watches Eddie, sitting across from her at the small table in the corner of the room, hoping for a positive reaction or response. His expression seems to be unchanging; even so, she continues with her best delivery, deciding it is the last portion of the story that should make or break his mood;

"So, what I guess, I'm trying to say is, even if we can't find Tim, we can always get a new one."

She pauses and looks to Eddie again, hoping the joke will take.

"Hell no! If we can't find Tim, I'm done. Don't find me any more brothers. I don't think I could handle another one."

He offers a smile to relieve his wife, about which he now realizes two things; she worries too much about him, as even in his most depressed moments, he's never had much trouble lightening up or taking a joke and secondly, that she apparently has no more emotional connection to animals than she would a handbag.

"So, a week? That's plenty enough time to move on and forget about your pet." Eddie adds mockingly.

"I didn't forget about her. It's just...it's a cat. She'd probably just become a stray, and it's not like there aren't plenty more of them out there."

"Damn...That's cold. I hope I never go missing. You'd remarry in a month."

"Two months tops, because I'd probably have to leave town to find a world-renowned Italian architect."

Jill offers a fittingly trenchant reply to her husband's sarcasm and continues smirking as she slyly introduces an agenda to her second response;

"It'd be different if it were my daughter."

Reaching out gently, Jill caresses Eddies arm.

"Jill...I'm sure when you finally meet my replacement, he'll be glad to give you children."

Eddie tries to keep the conversation flippant but knows this is likely to fail.

"That's not funny. You're giving me my daughter, damnit, even if I have to force it out of you."

Standing, Jill playfully slaps her palms upon the table.

"I'd think that was kinky, but...you're kind of scaring me right now."

Eddie chuckles and jumps back retreating behind his seat.

With hips gently swaying, Jill walks slowly and seductively around the table, stops and with a grin lunges out to grasp her husband who dodges but returns with similar efforts. Proceeding to seize her, Eddie then throws her down pinning her unto the nearby bed. With Eddie leaning over his wife they share a lustful stare with one another before they are interrupted;

"Hey! You freak-o pervs know I'm standing right here!"

Indeed, as he exclaims, Mike stands in the small rooms open doorway.

"Shit Mike, don't you knock?"

Eddie, who, caught up in the moment, had not actually seen the large man standing in the now open doorway, stands up as the blood quickly rushes into his face.

Jill sits up on the bed with her knees folded in front of her chest, clutching a blanket over her body, to prevent her nightwear from revealing too much to the intruder.

"How long have you been standing there?"

"I just got here, but, what the fuck? I've called your room like eight times. I thought we were going to go get something to eat."

"The phone didn't even ring, moron."

Jill tries to display her distaste for the interruption, but Michael, fundamentally, is oblivious.

"Yeah right, I figured you guys were gettin' it on."

"You figured that, but you decided to come over and not knock before coming in. Am I going to have to kick your ass Mike?"

Eddie returns to the table and his coffee.

"Well, I still figured I better check up and make sure somethin' didn't happen. I mean everyone else is disappearing an' shit...wait, what room is this?"

Mike turns to look at the large thirty-six clearly displayed on the still open door.

"Shit, no wonder, I thought you were in thirty-eight. Oh well, let's go get somethin' to eat. And thanks for covering up with that blanket Jill. Nothin' I wanna see."

Mike laughs, simultaneously dodging a flying shoe directed at his head.

■ 10:13ᴀᴍ

The Sunburst Motel in Wilbanks, Arizona features a small café aptly named The Sunburst Café. Its breakfast menu features a competent list of items including forty different types of omelets. However, its claim to fame, evidently, as the menu proudly proclaims, is 'The Ultimate Breakfast Burst', consisting of a massive five-egg cheddar, pepper jack and green chili omelet tightly wrapped around a copious mix of bacon, sausage, hash browns and gravy served with two large buttermilk biscuits. While Eddie and Jill consider a light breakfast to be perfectly fitting for the day ahead, Mike decides upon the profuse meal.

"You're nuts."

Jill mutters, shaking her head after Mike dispenses his order to an apparently disillusioned and likely hung-over waitress.

"All I can say is, you're paying for it. Seven damn dollars for an omelet." Eddie adds in between sips of what is now his fourth cup of coffee.

"Not just any omelet, it's *'The Best Omelet in Arizona'*. Plus it's got biscuits. An' I'm payin' for both of your grody-ass breakfasts too. It's my treat since you got dinner last night. An' since I'm payin' I can order whatever the hell I damn well please. You dinks."

Eddie, responding to Mike's short rant;

"Shut up dipshit. It's not like you didn't order the biggest steak you could find on the menu last night. I don't know how the hell you can put away food like that."

"That steak wasn't shit. You remember that steak thing they used to do at Morton's Ranch House, where if you eat the whole thing it's free—I did that like three times."

"That's not an achievement I'd go around bragging about… its things like that, that will keep you single. That, and the fact that your rancid feet give off a mile-wide smell."

"Nah, you just smell all the bullshit that comes out of your mouth. *Psych*."

Mike punctuates his sentence with a term he murmurs quickly and almost instinctively.

"No, don't start that. It took Ronnie and me forever to get them to stop saying that stupid word."

Jill protests and turns to look at Eddie, who interjects;

"I hardly ever said it."

"Yeah right, you and Tim both said it all the time. What the hell does 'psych' even mean?"

"I don't know, I think it means 'just kidding' or something. That's how I use it, anyways. Holy shit...Hell yeah."

The still despondent waitress places Mike's order before him and he quickly begins devouring the omelet with generous forkfuls.

"Yeah, well, don't start saying that either. You've never been serious with anything, so you'll be adding these stupid phrases like every time you speak."

Having received her order of toasted wheat and a bowl of oatmeal, Jill, too, begins eating, albeit, in much smaller portions leaving ample time between servings to allow for proper mastication and the, all too necessary, act of breathing.

"'Like' really? 'Like'...You sure?"

Mike chortles out the comment after eating another serving finishing off roughly one-third of the monstrous omelet.

"Shut up..."

Jill turns to her chuckling husband, apparently sharing Mike's humor and adds; "You too, butthead."

Eddie, eating his favored eggs and toast concoction; a 'Birds Nest' as he refers to it, has again vacated the conversation, mentally, and is partaking in another bout of deep thought.

"I've been thinking, not too many people seem to even know about this...tar. And the people who do, it's not like they have any idea what's going on. Not any more than we do. We could try finding someone who might know, but where the hell would we begin?"

A sip of coffee interjects before Eddie continues;

"I mean...Tim could have just disappeared, like Pete, and Ronnie now, but—I don't know. Maybe that's just bullshit... maybe we're just being stupid, and they're gone for good. Of course I hope not, and I don't want to stop looking, and I don't really want to even think that. I guess, maybe it just needs to be said; that we may never find them—Or Gramps. We could go back; I haven't been able to get a hold of Gramps..."

"You know Gramps. He's left, I'm sure, like Ronnie did. And they're not gone, Eddie, they're not dead. I know I can't be certain, but, this is just...too strange. You saw Ronnie. There was something more going on there. That black gunk or whatever you want to call it. I was watching it—it seemed like everything was bending into it; like giving into it. What Ronnie did was crazy. But I know you thought about doing it too."

Jill omits her own admission, but, even she, considered following Ronnie, and still does.

"Yeah and I saw that guy, or whatever the fuck he was, I ain't joking about that."

Michael's eyes flit back and forth between the couple while he piles the remainder of a large, gravy heaped biscuit into his mouth. He chews very briefly and swallows the majority before continuing with traces of the culinary conquest still meandering within his mouth.

"He jumped into that shit like he knew exactly what he was doing. But is that what we're talking about? Finding more of this crap to jump into...I don't know if I wanna go anywhere near that space ooze shit. Maybe if I get fuckin' ripped."

Moving his gaze from Jill Mike looks to Eddie, then looks down, donning a slightly dismayed look in response to the bareness of his plate.

"I've gotta make a call." Eddie returns to his feet and retrieves his wallet.

"Think again Cap-ee-tan! This one's on me, remember? Put that shit away."

Mike pulls out a small wad of cash and waves his hand at Eddie.

Jill watches her husband leave the restaurant. Mike takes note.

"Go ahead, Jill, I'm gonna buy a pack of cigarettes and I'll meet you guys at the room."

Back in room thirty-six; *not thirty-eight*, Jill sits at the edge of the now made bed with her hands folded and squeezed between her knees. Watching her husband fix his fingers into the old rotary-dial phone, she inquires;

"You calling your mom?"

"Yeah, I think I need to get this over with."

Eddie inhales deeply and lets out a short sigh.

■ 12:48PM

Barbara Chapel sits at her small desk just under a large window belonging to the decades-old Bowling Lane Real Estate office. Acting as a secretary for twenty-two years, she'd finally become an agent earlier in the month, and is proving very quickly, that her years of collected knowledge in the business of realty and her expert affability will soon make her one of the best. She only wishes the owner of the company, Bob Gladett, had realized this ten years ago, allowing her to retire much sooner. But as it stands, her goal of relatively early retirement should not be out of reach.

Her phone rings.

"Hello, this is Bowling Lane Real Estate, Barbara Chapel speaking."

"Mom?"

Eddie speaks with an odd uneasiness as he prepares to deliver the news to his mother. He is beginning to believe that not only will she, likely, never see her youngest son again, he's also become inclined to believe this would be the last conversation even he will ever share with her.

"Hi Eddie, so d'you find Tim?"

Barbara quickly drops the formal tone and replaces it with the warm and sincere quality to which Eddie is accustomed.

"Uh, no. Actually, Ronnie's gone now, too, and I think Gramps is."

Keeping the sentence simple, Eddie continues to contemplate how he will proceed explaining the entire affair.

"What? What the heck's going on? How—"

Eddie interrupts his mother;

"Well...I told you we thought Tim must've disappeared into that same stuff Gramps said Pete ran into. The tar or whatever it is. Well, we found more, and Ronnie—we couldn't even react quick enough to stop her. She just walked right into it."

"Why would she do that? What's wrong with that girl?"

Barbara sighs and places her palm to her head as she begins to surmise the aim of the conversation.

"I don't know, I guess she thought, since that's how Tim disappeared, the only way to find him, would be to follow him."

Keeping as composed as possible, Eddie can sense, and attempts to avoid, the frustration beginning to surface on the other end of the phone.

"Well you're not doing that. I know you want to find your brother, and I want him back, but I don't want both of my sons missing, Eddie. I don't know what's going on here, but maybe we should contact somebody, call emergency, figure out what's going on before jumping into anything...literally!"

"I called the cops Mom, I told you that. They're aware of it, but they don't have any idea what the hell's going on. Not any more than we do. I don't think anybody does."

Eddie decides to redirect the conversation, if only temporarily.

"And Gramps, I've tried to reach him, I don't know, probably six times so far, I can't get a hold of him. Maybe when you're off, could you swing by his house and find out what's going on?

I guess I should call the police and report Ronnie as missing. Maybe report Gramps too."

"I'll look Eddie, and I'll call the police, and let them know about Ronnie and if Norm's not home, I'll let them know about him as well. But maybe you and Jill should head back. Maybe we were wrong in reacting so quickly, now that more people are disappearing, maybe you should come back home until we know more about what's going on."

The realization haunts Barbara, even as she speaks, that her words will fall on deaf ears.

"Mom, I'm not coming back. Not until I find Tim. I'd like to think that we'll eventually find out what's happening and maybe he'll show up, but I just...I'm going to find him. He'd do the same if it was me."

"I'm not losing both of my boys."

Barbara's welling emotions are becoming increasingly obvious as it distorts her voice.

"I love you Mom."

Eddie manages to conceal similar emotions, but maintains the great sincerity of the sentiment.

"Eddie...come home."

This statement is hardly demanding, and resonates instead with an expression of both love and despair that, though sounding sincere, implies the existence of a greater desire subduing her dismay. Saying what she wanted her son to hear, she ultimately wishes for him to continue his search, in hopes that he would return to her, with his brother.

"I love you too, Eddie. Stay away from that stuff causing all this trouble. And when you find Tim, tell him I love him. Then bring his ass back here." She then forces herself to laugh and lighten the moment as best she can.

"I will Mom, I'll see you soon...bye."

Eddie decides not to consider this a lie, as the truth of the statement remains to be determined, but he has growing doubts he will ever return to Bowling, or again, see any of its citizens.

"Goodbye Eddie." His mother does not.

Mike swings open the hotel room door just as Eddie replaces the phone upon the receiver. Eddie looks up at Mike, who beams a dually excited and panicked expression across his sweating face.

"Mike! What the hell?! Didn't I tell you about that this morning. Knock on the damn door, and we'll let you in when we are prepared to deal with your shit."

A shrug traverses through Eddies shoulder as he turns his hands at his sides with his palms facing Michael, as if expressing the same dismay already revealed in words.

"Chill out. You're both fully clothed, but fuck it. Look I found some more of that tar shit just behind the hotel office. I don't know what your plans are, but that craps not gonna stick around forever."

Mike pants out the hurried words and begins heaving deeply trying to recover his breaths.

"What'd you run over here for? Why don't you sit down for a second? You look like you're about to die."

Without so much concern as patronization, Jill speaks and gestures.

Regardless of her sentiment, Mike heeds her recommendation and sits at the end of the bed, slowly managing to regain composure.

■ 1:01PM

Behind the hotel office, weeds grow profusely along the walls and the chain-link fence surrounding the back portion of the property. Several groupings of dead grass, cradling various bits of litter, blemish the earth and accompany the decaying relics of the not-so-distant past; including an old sun-rotted truck tire, rusted metal buckets, empty paint cans, and an old truck axle cracked along the center and almost completely rusted through.

Just beyond this axle edging out from the hotel towards the chain-link fence, as Mike claimed they would, the party finds the increasingly familiar pool of obsidian black. This consortium of dark matter is far larger than those the group previously encountered and Eddie estimates is around twelve feet in diameter.

Eddie looks to his wife with an expression both revealing his intentions and questioning her's.

She replies in words; "You know I'll follow you, Eddie, it's your decision."

"Shit, you know what? I'm up for it. Better than wasting time like we've been doing, driving around on some bogus journey to nowhere. At least we might figure out what the fuck's up with all this bullshit goin' on."

Mike edges closer to the material and continues; "Besides, I can't get ripped 'cause I ain't got anymore weed."

Staring into the vast, malevolent darkness, Mike awaits a response.

"It could mean death. I hope that's occurred to you Mike. We could be out of our damned minds and just taking a giant leap off a cliff."

Eddie reaches in front of him and grasps Mike's shoulder pulling him back slightly.

"Nah man, it's like a leap of faith. We jump off a cliff and land in a river or some shit. We jump and we figure out where Tim's gone. And if we're wrong, I don't know...we're all wrong together, and it's not gonna mean shit to us. It's everybody else who's gonna have to deal with the funerals."

"Well, you'll be burning in hell."

Turning to Mike, Jill snickers in response to her own statement.

"And like I said, we'll all be together."

"No, I'll see if we can schedule visits in heaven. Maybe they'll send you to purgatory so we can see you for an hour, and we'll bring lunch or something. Otherwise, you're all alone on that one."

Eddie steps forward beside Mike and shares the same vacant stare into the tar.

"You guys really think I'm going to hell?"

Looking up, Mike reveals an expression of concern, the first Eddie's seen in some time.

"Come on Mike, you can take a joke...anyways, only time will tell."

Eddie slaps Mike's shoulder, pauses and takes in a deep breath, continuing; "So I guess, this is it. Are we set?"

NUMBERS FOR NAMES (DULLED BY EXCESS)

■ 9:01PM SEPTEMBER 3RD 2176

    The primary traffic and overall action within the city appears to take place at the suspended tiers, upon the first of which, Ronnie now currently resides, along with thousands of other pedestrians and vehicles. It bustles in nauseating momentum just before her, as the excess of chaotic flashing lights and noise dulls her senses. She can't imagine how long one could go on living in a place like this without becoming completely lost and dulled in its overabundance.

    The vehicle traffic blasts by with overwhelming speeds and the foot traffic appears largely regulated as paths littered with directing arrow animations and lights traverse alongside every street and building. Like walkways between airport terminals, directions indicate thousands of different options to keep the pedestrian traffic constant and managed between destinations, discouraging any potential wanderlust. She decides upon a course and starts to her left following the path alongside the street apparently known as two 'R' dash twenty-four. All of the street names appear to follow this seemingly incoherent convention and bear monikers constructed of what Ronnie sees as a random grouping of letters and numbers. She assumes they must have some meaning, but then again, she never really understood the naming conventions used to designate the streets in Bowling, supposing most of Bowling's street names were simply names of founders.

Or some meaningless phrases meant to sound western, like Bonnie's Gulch or Prairie Pass.

At least, she thinks, it would be much easier giving and receiving directions in Bowling, rather than in a place where the directions must sound like instructions on filing tax forms.

TabSurf not functioning and you need directions? Follow 2R-24 to 1014D-12 (16.32 km); continue along 1014D-12 (9.63 km) and use section B at the 614-CT transfer; end in 2.11 km as 1014CT-12 intersects CL56.

Reading this below an advertisement for what Ronnie assumes is some kind of bar, instructing the manual method in which to find the location of the HalcyON Public Lounge, Ronnie decides this may be as good a location as any to begin her search and follows the dry, technical directions. Although not entirely sure what the instructions mean, what a Public Lounge is, or even a TabSurf, Veronica figures she'll wing it and wind up somewhere indoors, if only to get away from the streets.

Ronnie spends four minutes walking along two 'R' dash twenty-four before she arrives at the intersecting ten-fourteen 'D' dash twelve. She'd found the walk to be very brisk, and much of the speed did not seem to be of her own production, it was as if the strange pellucid walkway had somehow sped her along. She couldn't complain, as it means much less effort on her part. But she finds that with every increasingly contrasting curiosity she discovers in this world, the more unsettled she becomes. And it strikes her with some significance, how the entire environment seems to be inclined to rob pedestrians of much control.

Arriving at the crosswalk indicated in the directions, Ronnie pauses for a moment.

The directions, she remembers, indicate that she would need to cross two 'R' dash twenty-four to continue travelling north along ten-fourteen 'D' dash twelve. She wonders at the site of the speeding traffic, how she could possibly get across. And with that thought, traffic is immediately halted as the crosswalk lights up, and though she does not move her feet or legs, Veronica finds herself darting across the street with little time to even contemplate the process. Ronnie turns back and looks at the street she'd just inexplicably crossed, from what she could estimate; she'd travelled across seven lanes of traffic in less than two seconds. And no sooner than having turned around, the traffic is flowing, once more, at incredible speed.

She returns to face the recommended direction and begins walking north while shaking her head, trying to make sense of several disturbing thoughts.

How did I make it across that crosswalk without actually WALKING? Why didn't I fall flat on my ass if I was flying so quickly across? And why did every stupid car stop in that perfectly uniform pattern as soon as I'd reached the crosswalk?

Whatever.

Ronnie continues walking and decides that either she'll be in this place long enough to find the answers to these questions and probably wish she had never even bothered with the questions, or she'll find Tim and they'll gladly make their way home, at which point, she'll realize she couldn't care less about how this world operates.

Yeah right, fat chance of that happening.

She doesn't expect the latter to be the case.

Twelve miles!?

Ronnie estimates with some quick calculation based on what the advertisement stated, she's somehow walked twelve miles in six minutes. With only four remaining she decides to stop again. Half expecting to be shot across the walkway as she was at the crosswalk, she finds herself almost disappointed. Though, when she walks she feels propelled, when she stops, she finds herself standing motionless with what she expects is a stupidly expectant look on her face.

It must just be the crosswalks that move you automatically...I guess. All the other walkways just help speed things along.

She begins walking once more.

The remaining four miles are traversed quickly as Ronnie looks around surveying the city. Most of the buildings stretch virtually unending into the charcoal sky and are surrounded, intersected and supported several floors above by more of the same floating street tiers. She can only assume that the walkways are actually physical, if almost entirely transparent, while the streets are merely projections used for guiding traffic, as the vehicles appear to have little issue flying through the sky. Though Ronnie is nearly accurate in her assumption, in truth, the vehicles do not fly, but are supported magnetically through rails set within the walkways.

The buildings have the same structure and design as she'd noted at floor level; it looks to her as if the different sections composing each building could shift, rotate and move at any given moment. Although each building varies in shape and size, they all appear to be constructed of the same material in largely the same fashion, with their most distinguishing features being the bright multitude of both static and animated three-dimensional commercial projections.

Observing the other foot traffic, that making the continuous noise of empty chatter, Veronica notes the extremely odd appearance of the majority.

The most common choices in apparel for the majority of these strange citizens composed of strikingly small and thin individuals, appearing in an unusually broad array of skin-colors, seems to be near-skintight, brightly-lined, synthetic outfits of various shapes and sizes, all excessively cluttered with printed advertisements; some of these even appear animated. The multitude of skin colors appear to be superficial, and often in abstract designs like full-body makeup or paint.

A few of the minor variations in clothing accessories include; exaggerated collars extending to the shoulders and stretching down at one side like the end of a scarf, strange over-shirts open in the front which appear to be short in the abdomen and lacking arm length, and the strangest accessory Ronnie notices to be prevalent are facemasks which cover the nose and mouth and come to a sharp point in the vertical center of the face resembling a beak.

Her desire for anonymity is at conflict with her casual outfit, naturally light-brown skin and brown features, clashing greatly with the superficial and synthetic choices prominent within the city. She suddenly feels very self-conscious, but it passes as she considers that fitting in with these crowds should truly be the least of her desires.

Whatever happened to a T-shirt and a pair of jeans?

Her current outfit.

Completing the exact distance noted in the HalcyON advertisement, Veronica discovers what'd been referred to as the transfer. It is nothing like she'd expected, which was something along the lines of a fork in the road or a freeway exit. Instead, the transfer is a split station featuring a system of elevating tubes which transport both vehicle and foot traffic to various locations above the current street level. Craning her neck upwards, Ronnie watches as several vehicles are rapidly propelled sky-high to other street tiers above her, noticing that the platforms carrying the traffic arrive in multitudes and seem to be available as soon as a vehicle or pedestrian arrives.

Entering the station, she is taken aback by the size, or lack thereof. It certainly looked small from the outside, but is absolutely cramped on the inside, with at least seven platform sections confined into a capacity just large enough to allow the most precise of vehicle movements required to enter and exit each platform. Ronnie remembers a Japanese man who'd she once served at The Quartz. In a conversation they'd shared, he described what he called capsule hotels in Osaka, which were designed at a minimal two-meter capacity shelved in tall buildings with rooms just large enough to fit a small bed. She imagines this city must be facing a much greater scale of overpopulation.

At least, Ronnie considers, everything in this peculiar city is clearly labeled. Signs designating the routes to each section hover and blink in various areas throughout the transfer terminal. She finds the entryway to section 'B' and waits in line to the left of the vehicle traffic entrance, in the clearly marked entrance division intended for pedestrian traffic. Four people stand ahead of her and one behind; all are standing in uncomfortable proximity.

Veronica can hear the conversation between two of the people in front of her as they periodically look back at her and flash berating smirks. She figures she may be offended if she could only understand half of the words they are using as they spit out evidently common urban colloquialisms like; "She delphine, but licks them dreads." and, "Skeeps those croths. Verideous."

The overtly effeminate emphasis provided by the obviously male voices issuing these phrases makes them all-the-more exasperating and Ronnie decides to remain silent, ignoring as much of the environment as she can manage for the time being.

Most would credit Veronica for her social ambitions, and her ability to spark up a conversation with just about anyone, but even someone as outgoing as her would be forgiven for not obliging in whatever social conventions this obstinately strange world offers.

She only hopes that not every person in the city speaks this same vernacular.

If so, this day's just going to drag on, because I'm not speaking to any of these weirdos.

A few fleeting moments pass.

The seemingly awkward Ronnie follows the lead of the pseudo-men just before her and steps into the small platform chamber. As soon as she stops, the surface below her feet takes notice and responds shooting her skywards several hundred feet in a matter of seconds, she nearly falls to the platform but manages to position her stance and keep her balance. Peering through the platform Ronnie watches as distance quickly builds between her and the station beneath. She feels nauseated as she considers the remarkably thin and nearly invisible, glass-like platform which is the only object supporting her at the great heights she finds herself ascending rapidly and with no noticeable discretion.

Deciding to redirect her attention, she turns to the horizon, or where she suspects it would be. She remembers that it would be impossible to see anything beyond the hundreds of distractingly decorated buildings intent on concealing the outer world from all of those unfortunate enough to be stuck within this dismal city, as oblivious they may be. Still, she looks onward.

If there even is a world beyond this city, the people here surely wouldn't know, or maybe would forget after a few minutes spent here being railed by these mind-numbing displays.

Ronnie wonders how many people in this city question such things. They all seem oddly content with the constant jading tumultuousness distributed by the barrage of animated visuals and sounds broadcasting from virtually every surface, the claustrophobic smothering provided by the crowded street systems and profuse development, and the overall desensitizing of the entire chaotic environment to which Ronnie fears, she will never become accustomed. And by no means does she desire to enter the state of mind that allows her such adaptation.

"I hate this place." She insists, sighing while gently whispering the words. Ronnie arrives at the third street tier and exits the transfer station onto ten-fourteen C-T dash twelve.

■ 9:22PM

HalcyON Public Lounge is displayed in a somewhat modest style featuring a minimalist white on black design and a very small line in the corner indicating the owner of the institution; *Omni Networks*, with the 'O' and 'N' emphasized in the same textual design as fashioned into the lounge's name. Appearing larger at first as Ronnie nears the establishment, she finds this to be some kind of optical trick with the sign reducing to a size smaller than the width of the entrance on approach. It doesn't appear to be a sign constructed of any physical substance, but is merely a projection appearing to sway in gentle wave-like movements while suspended between two small frames on both the left and right sides.

It beats the hell out of that gaudy eyesore hanging over The Quartz.

Greeted by two thin swinging doors of a semi-transparent blue-hued metal, Ronnie can not only see the mass of crowds providing surprisingly subdued interior activity, but can see the translucent digital postings which advertise all of the wonderful times to be had at upcoming events held within the apparently popular HalcyON Public Lounge. One of the acts displayed catches Ronnie's attention; known as DisktWerX, they look to Ronnie like silver cyborgs wearing some kind of tall cylindrical digital helmets labeled 'D-W-X' and dark, but lustrous suits scattered with numerical designs and bar graphs breaking up the otherwise slate-grey coloring.

A button on the illusory door beckons with the words *'hear and see'*; she pushes her finger into the cold metal and though she does not feel any indication of reaction, the swinging doors become opaque and the display becomes animated, playing a sample of the band's musical performance. As the recorded band plays their strange flat-top instrument surfaces suspended before them, the numbers and bars displayed across their unusual dark clothing begin to move in a rhythm corresponding with the sounds as, equally odd, but far less clothed women appear to dance in the background.

If you can call that flailing around and weirdo body jerks dancing. It's more like a combination of seizure and a clumsy orgasm.

She 'sees and hears' for a short period in amazement at the doors ability to not only project an incredible enveloping sound, but also managing to mute all other sound from the city for the moment while it plays the rapid music. It is as if the door is modifying the physical nature of sound itself. As she continues to marvel, Ronnie notes that the music is completely alien, bearing no similarity to anything she's ever heard before, every sound and ambient noise produced is unique to her, but strangely compelling and at times she finds it to be incredibly rhythmic.

It doesn't look like there's any dancing going on inside. They're not even doing that lame spazoid body-jerk junk from the video.

Ronnie assumes similar music would be playing inside and as she redirects her gaze to peer through the doors they become transparent once more. Through the portion of the door not still displaying the video, Veronica observes the occupants for a moment before entering HalcyON.

Ronnie walks into the establishment and is greeted by the same peculiar aural phenomena. She can hear nothing outside of the surrounding music emanating from unknown locations. The sleek interior of the public lounge is a combination of white and silver hues with illuminated accents and trims of various flashing and changing colors; videos project, disbanded, from nearly every wall. The ceiling appears completely animated with a remarkable, surreal display of stars both shooting across the sky and at various times exploding creating expanding universes with vibrant shifting nebulas and holographic planets orbiting around the entire lounge. She stares at the ceiling for what feels like several minutes, but the animation does not appear to repeat itself in any way or follow any sort of pattern, creating the illusion of natural and chaotic universal occurrences.

The Quartz with its tacky neon shapes and prints of tropical scenes and exotic cars would look totally lame compared to this place.

The place is crowded, more so than The Quartz on its busiest of weekends, but, in fairness, the capacity of The Quartz couldn't sustain even half of the crowd present within the HalcyON.

The occupants seem more inclined to stay seated as only a few of the patrons are standing, and of those, Ronnie notices only one making movement in response to the music. Again, not dancing, she considers the short haphazard sways and simple head bobbing to be lacking in any enthusiasm, appearing similar to the dazed movements of someone mesmerized by a form of hypnosis rather than dancing. This dancing man, or whatever it is, she thinks, should do as little as possible to draw attention to himself. The comical, dancing, quasi-male looks to be nearly six-feet, five-inches tall and is of far greater girth than any citizen she's seen thus far. Ronnie suspects he must weigh nearly three-hundred pounds. And though she feels the individual's gender is likely male, she is perplexed by his heavy, silver-blue eyeshadow sharply contouring into strange shapes and extending beyond the thin black-bar shaped shades resting along his nose. A small, perfectly round patch of jet black hair sits at the very top of the otherwise bald neo-man and his clothes are not unlike the others she's seen, but the strange extended collar appears even more exaggerated in his flamboyantly bright uniform. He doesn't appear to have taken to the disturbing beak mask she'd seen others wearing, but she'd almost prefer it to the matching silver-blue and black lipstick and line-work drawn along his synthetically white colored cheeks.

Give me a break!

This man, of sorts, has apparently gone through some great lengths to try to fit in with a city full of uniformly bizarre beings, probably trying to compensate for his abundant size.

Veronica quickly realizes she is staring at the man and decides that because she cannot tell if he's noticed due to his black shades, she should redirect her attention elsewhere.

Ronnie finds only one table remains unused and decides to seat herself. The surprisingly comfortable seat is supported by a single small, transparent pillar which expands fluidly into the curved ergonomic shape of the seat. The seat is completely white and highly reflective aside from the glowing line work wrapping around its circumference and expanding towards the top in a design similar to circuitry. The table before her is suspended from the ceiling by another transparent column designed in a similar fashion to that of the seat. The animated astronomical display appears to flow from the top of the lounge, bleeding down through the posts suspending the tables to the ceiling. Three-dimensional holographic panels project from the table surface just in front of each seat at a forty-five degree angle, each providing a list of features which include access to free and sample audio and video channels, a purchasing section for buying premium audio and video channels, channels for both free and 'premium' digital gaming, access to what is referred to as the 'OmniNet', access to the food and drink menu, and an assistance option evidently used to request assistance in the event of any unforeseeable issues.

Veronica can find no one who appears to be employed by the lounge; no bartender, wait staff, or host. Service, it seems, is provided entirely through the projected displays. This being the case, Ronnie decides to operate the terminal before her in an attempt to order a drink. After a few minutes spent pressing her fingers through the projection, she finds herself capable enough to find the drink menu. Browsing through the enormous collection of drinks, the majority of which are completely unknown to her, Ronnie finds her preferred cocktail, a modest rum and coke. In the HalcyON lounge it is referred to as *'The Tripol-C'*, or Carbonated Coca Cane, *because it would just be too damned difficult to simply say rum and coke or even Cuba Libre.* Ronnie, however recognizes most of the artificial ingredients as those listed in her simple beverage and places her order. Unfortunately, the display opens a small prompt stating that a Cred-I-D number is required, and because Veronica Raquel Rawls should be deceased, feeding the soil and its inhabitants for over one-hundred years, or otherwise non-existent by the year twenty-one, seventy-six, she figures any number associated with her name would not work.

So much for that idea.

Resting her head into her hand, Ronnie stares at the panel, flicking her fingers through the display, listlessly, rifling through countless menus and quietly determining where she should begin with her amateur investigation.

Just behind her a masculine voice, making feeble attempts to mimic feminine tones, speaks to her;

"Girl, what is that hor-ideous croths you scourtin'? You too delphine to be donin' dreads like that."

Veronica fights the urge to turn around and meet, let alone greet the individual for fear that it may belong to any individual even remotely similar to the assumed depiction developing in her mind.

She gives in and turns around responding;

"Croths? Delphine? What the hell are you talking about?"

The incredibly large and awkward man Ronnie noticed dancing only minutes before, now stands just behind her seat and replies;

"I'm sorry swang; that was rude of me. *Introductions*; I am Gnuella and croths are clothes and I just have to say, yours are dreadful. Dreadful threads, *dreads*."

The words *'introductions'* and *'dreads'* ring out in rapid pace and especially high peals with Gnuella's intention to provide emphasis. Ronnie finds the manner strange, if not considerably irritating.

"Oh, and Delphine, is a fine lady, like you'sef."

Ronnie assumes this means she's considered attractive, and it disturbs her greatly, when considering the beholder who's provided the compliment.

Finding herself wishing, now more than ever, to be home in the comfort of familiar surroundings with people of simple presentation and intention, the sudden fervent dread of possible things to come sinks deep into her body and extends into her arms and legs. She sits, motionless, for a moment with no intention of continuing the conversation, or committing any action whatsoever, until she can once again regain her thoughts and composure.

"Let me buy you that drink." Gnuella leans over, whispers the words and summons through Ronnie's console, an animated spinning image of the carbonated coca cane.

With a couple of quick presses into the panel and a wave of the wrist over some kind of small scanner installed in the table Gnuella orders a rum and coke and something called a *'Bre Pristano'*; a concoction comprised of Rum, a refined compound similar to a mix of grenadine and dry vermouth, and an artificial pineapple flavoring. Ronnie can only hope this is the only round of drinks she will be sharing with the man. She also hopes, given the circumstances, that this particular rum and coke is made with premium rum, in great quantity. At least, she figures, this would render the situation a bit more bearable.

Just beyond the display, the center of the table opens and two drinks ascend to the surface and are transported to the area between her seat and the seat across from her, where Gnuella has landed his large body. She waits for him to retrieve his drink, as with the oddly shaped and opaque bottles she finds no traditional way of distinguishing the two. Gnuella retrieves the taller, lighter-colored bottle and leaves what must be the rum and coke; Ronnie reaches out to grasp the bottle, but Gnuella beats her to it and pulls it playfully to himself, just out of her reach.

Given that she's found very little serenity since the moment of her arrival in this bemusing city and that each following moment has only enforced her dismay and pressed her to become more cynical, with this man's playful little gesture, Ronnie can immediately feel frustration boil to the surface of her face and she finds herself on the verge of creating a very uncomfortable situation. However, she reasons that any kind of harsh reaction which she may normally be inclined to allow herself would amount to only trouble in a place where she is not only unaccustomed, but where she has no allies to speak of. She quickly decides to wait a moment and allows herself to calm.

"You want it, keep it. You paid for it, anyways."

Ronnie smirks as she verbally bats away the annoyance.

Gnuella pushes the drink back, and apologizes;

"Sorry Cheello. So spills, why you so low? "

"Look, I'm not from around here. In fact, I just got here today, and I'm sorry but I don't really know what you're saying, and I'm not really here looking for...conversation, or whatever you're shooting for, so thanks for the drink, but I'm not really interested."

"It's no b'ang Cheello, just a drink, but...why come to a place like this, if you ain't lookin' for comp'? Where you from anyhow?"

"I—I'm from, a small town not very near here. And I'm actually here looking for someone, if you really need to know."

Ronnie retrieves the rum and coke, deciding that humoring the man's questions is enough to warrant it hers. She sips from the small open hole at the top of the neck and grimaces at the almost unbearably sweet taste followed by a strangely synthetic aftertaste.

"A small town? Wait, you mean like an unreq zone? Shailao! Keep that to you'sef, cheello, you could get in some s'real shrib if an A-M-A ass-hole-shiate hears that." Gnuella leans into the table and whispers almost frantically.

"I don't understand *ANYTHING* you're saying. Unreq? And why the hell do you keep calling me a *chee-low*?" Ronnie finds her arm raising the bottle to her face now agape anticipating another sip, but she halts both actions immediately, recalling the taste. She replaces the bottle on the table, and closes her mouth.

I wonder if the water tastes like plastic too.

Gnuella bears a slight stern look on his face and leans in further, closing in on the preoccupied Ronnie; "Follow me."

"*Uhm*...I don't think so, in fact, thanks for the drink, but I really need to leave."

Ronnie stands hurriedly and readies to race to the exit.

"Wait! A cheello is something like a foreigner or denizen, like an obviously misplaced person. *You*. An unreq, or unrequistioned zone is an area that has not yet been acquired by an ascosite – It's like a city with a localized government oriented around an association and its subsidiaries. We are in an ascosite, one of the largest, in fact. A-M-A associates are Ascosite Mandated Authorities, and they vigilantly watch for discrepancies. Again, *you*. And you're right, you do need to leave, but you probably have nowhere to go, and it may be considerably ill-advised for you to do so alone. So, if you are not still frightened, you may follow me. I may be able to help you find who you're looking for, but if this person has a brain in their head, you will not find them here."

Though Gnuella rapidly fires the response in whispered tones, Ronnie notes the remarkably coherent, deep, assertive yet sanguine voice Gnuella uses. She is startled by the sudden contradiction in his demeanor, but considers it to be a vast improvement.

Ronnie's initial cynicism dictates a refusal, but she considers her lack of options and tries to build a mental collection of worst-case scenarios revolving around the choice of staying in the noisy club and ultimately being stranded in an undesirable place, never finding any proper way to proceed, in addition to never being able to find a decent drink; or following the unusually large, and apparently split-persona man to either her peril, death or some safe-place bearing a revelation of some sort. Veronica quiets her thoughts for a short moment, briefly looks around the room and makes her decision.

"If it gets me out of here, then let's go...I guess."

SOMEWHAT DAMAGED (I, ROBOT)

■ DATE AND TIME IN QUESTION

The greater portion of his life, Norman served in the work force as a painter. He'd started painting at a young age while working as a gas attendant in a full service auto station. After a couple of years of loyal dedication pumping gas and cleaning windows, he was asked to assist in body work and found a passion in painting, eventually allowing the station to add custom paintjobs to their repertoire, courtesy of the young artist. Due to this natural talent, it was only a short matter of time before he became widely known in the small town of Bowling for his painting skills.

His abilities were not restricted to vehicles, however, as roughly half of the businesses in town, at one time or another, featured a Norman Donaldson masterpiece painted upon their windows, hanging in their stores or restaurants, or serving as wall-sized murals featuring bikinied women straddling classic cars, in the case of Speedy's bar.

After serving in World War II, he returned to Bowling to greet enough success to allow early retirement at the age of forty-one. He then resigned himself to being a dedicated husband, car enthusiast, and world traveler until the later years of his life after his wife Virginia passed away. This resulted in Norman's only time spent travelling to consist of short trips to the store, restaurant, or bar.

During his later years, it was rare for Norman to take up the brush and, in fact, by the time the Chapel brothers were born,

*the famous painter, Norman Donaldson, had become something
of a lost legend. No one knew for certain why he'd all but given
up the paint; some speculated it was the result of Virginia's
demise, or his crowning achievement on Speedy's wall having
burned away in an electrical fire. In Norman's mind it was simple; over twenty years had he associated paint with work, and
after all of those years filled with often daunting lengths of time
spent painting, he'd grown weary of it. He'd often thought; after
a long enough period of time he might one day take it up again
as a hobby, but the desire never seemed to rekindle.*

Lying in such terrible pain on what he feels to be cold metal
with his eyes closed so tight he finds himself reluctant to try to
open them, oddly enough, Norman can think only of painting.
The weight of the strokes, the admiration of the public, the absolute control of everything from perspective to color and the
ability to bring a detailed thought into the physical visual realm.
These were the things he'd allowed himself to forget in light of
the begrudging aspects of his work; those often upset clients
who would tear apart his ideas only to replace them with their
hideous, contrived desires, the terribly long hours spent to create such work that would ultimately be plagued with criticism,
too often his own.

And the pay, he'd never complained and he'd given every
client the best of his abilities and while, with many it would
be aptly compensated, it didn't make it any easier or any less
insulting when those few would short-change him.

But the thoughts find themselves growing now in his mind;
the strange tinge of inspiration is suddenly reborn in his heart
for the first time in thirty-one years. He supposes now, that this
was the primary reason he'd stopped painting, he'd lost the
ambition of his youth, whether through complacency, or fulfill-
ment. Now it begins to burn within him; it has transformed him
somehow, aroused, perhaps, by the need to find his lost friends
and, possibly, for the final time in his life, prove his worth once

more. It is the great, last motivation and desire building into full fruition and taking total control of his mind and body. Its final return is welcome.

Norman's eyes open slowly. Very little light illuminates the room, but it's just enough to allow him to view his surroundings. The large room is constructed of rough looking steelwork clearly showing its age. In various sections of his surroundings Norman makes out a collection of containers resembling oversized train cars, long cylindrical tanks, and various sizes of metal crates; all with panels on various sides and some with working lighted displays projected from the panels. A storage room, one that hasn't been used, or even likely seen, for some time, with walls of brown and grey, thick with rust and dirt. Norman can smell the decaying metal particles in the air.

His motivation falters with the cloying artificial atmosphere as he peers through the darkness and breathes in the age of the strange room and can feel the old familiar pains burgeoning in his head and bones.

Though Norman realizes the spark hasn't completely dispersed, he is left with flickering embers, and little more than the urge to leave wherever it is he currently finds himself.

Ambition, it seems to Norman, is always easier to muster, when not facing reality.

A great deal of effort is summoned and Norman can feel the aches and stabs zipping through his limbs and joints as he stands. It's almost too overwhelming and he quickly leans over bracing himself with his left arm on a nearby metal crate which stands, thankfully, at a height just above his knees. The containers surface is cold to the touch and from the quick impact of his weight falling through his arm into the crate, he discovers it to be both strong and rigid, and fortunately so. He raps on the crate and it makes so little noise he assumes it must have exceptionally thick interior walls, if it is not solid all the way through. He can only imagine how much it weighs. These containers are obviously well-constructed with intention for abundantly securing the contents inside, but none appear to be opened. Placed in storage and forgotten, for what Norman believes be many years.

The oddities of both the room and situation strike the old man suddenly, as if his faculties have only just completed their recovery after waking from the horrible stupor. It was only just moments ago that he'd been in his garage, and now, he finds himself somewhere completely unlike his garage, or Bowling, or anywhere he'd ever known to exist, surrounded by vast containers with lighted panels displaying technology he's never seen the likes of.

"What in th' hell's goin' on here? I'm too old for this crap."

A needless soliloquy echoes lightly in the lifeless room.

Taking a seat on a short metal crate, Norman rests for a moment hoping to gather some strength or at the very least recover the remainder of his faculties, enough to proceed. How he will proceed is completely unapparent to him, at the moment. He looks around once more in an attempt to find any form of exit from the building within which he finds himself trapped. Nothing of the sort appears in his immediate view. Norman proceeds to walk throughout the storage room between towers of crates and walls of containers, climbing over the shorter ones with grunts and, with groans, sidling beside the large ones where areas become too thin. After several minutes of exhaustive searching, Norman finds no exit.

He gruffly shouts; "Dammit all."

And receives an entirely unexpected response.

A voice from some unseen location within the room replies in an artificial sounding, zealous, somewhat sinewy and strangely-accented manner, Norman places somewhere between British and German;

"How may I assist you sir?"

"Who's there? Show yourself dammit!" Startled by the response, Norman looks frantically around the room.

THROUGH **DIMENSIONAL DETOURS**   133

From behind three precariously stacked, mid-sized crates hovers a diminutive robotic figure of roughly two feet in height bearing a perfectly round and mostly featureless head with two solid lights resembling eyes.

"I am sorry to have startled you. I am LumTechs Model Y-R-S dash F-N forty-two. You may call me Yursfon if you prefer, as some tend."

"What the hell are you supposed to be? Where in God's name am I?"

"I am an automated sub-facility assistance drone designed for inventory management, and general assistance in all Prictex Premium[ebr] sub-facilities. We are currently located within the Prictex Premium[ebr] Energy and Travel Service Center three, thirty-four, alpha storage unit fourteen—May I ask you sir, have I offended you somehow? Judging by your vocal tones and facial distortions, I believe I must have. Would you prefer another vocal pattern or accent?"

Norman waves his hand lightly, "Nah, forget it. Makes no damn difference. With all this crazy crap, no voice change could make it any better. I'm talkin' to a damn toaster."

"I see sir. Do you require further assistance?" The robotic creature rotates its head sideways as if to further express the questioning form.

"Stop calling me 'sir' dammit. If you gotta call me somethin', call me 'Gramps'. And yeah, I need *'assistance'*, how'm I supposed to get outta here?"

"*Gramps*? That name cannot be found within our employment database. Is this perhaps a nickname?"

"Yeah, but I ain't an employee of nothin'. I don't even know how'n the hell I got here."

Norman slowly and cautiously approaches the robot with a child-like curiosity.

"I see. Unfortunately, I do not know how you could have arrived at this location, within alpha storage unit fourteen, having not used the entrance, and I must admit, it did perplex me some to find you here without the initiation of proper unit entrance clearance protocols within my databanks, as was last recorded twelve years, three days and sixteen minutes past. However, if you wish to leave, please follow and I will direct you to the exit."

Gramps watches the small robot move at a rapid pace through various crates and containers. He hesitates for a short moment, but this short moment is just enough for the automated being to disappear out of the elderly mans limited field of view.

"Godammit, I can't walk that fast. Where the hell'd you get off to?"

The robot returns within seconds in a manner decidedly similar to the moment when he'd first revealed himself and even repeats;

"How may I assist you *Gramps*?" With the word Gramps bearing an entirely different tone, as if added to a prerecorded statement.

"I can't move that fast, you dumb bucket of bolts, slow down so I can see where yer goin'."

Gramps hobbles towards the robot in the quickest pace comfortable enough not to send sharp pains shooting through his legs and lower back.

"My damned hips actin' up again, too. So just slow the hell down, would'ya?"

"Do you require medical assistance, *Gramps*?"

"No, I do not. Just keep movin' – but go slow, so I can keep up with ya. *Yurrie*."

Gramps nicknames the artificial creature mimicking the strange tonal offset applied to his own name previously.

At a manageable pace the miniature machine leads Norman through a winding route between towers of giant cargo boxes climbing over randomly scattered crates and in one particularly painful moment Norman is forced to duck under a massive container supported across short crates.

"Ah shit!"

Norman halts quickly and slumps to the ground clutching his lower back while bending over.

The android, having been just short enough to pass under the container, does so once more and doubles back to assist the old man. Standing just in front of Norman in an almost disconcerting silence, the robot begins to emit several crossing beams of light from its center. The lattice of thin green lasers climbs over Norman's body in quick, geometrically specific patterns before disappearing back into the little automatons body.

"Biological scans indicate acute dystrophy in the labrum and femoral head, compression of the sciatic nerve in addition to senile osteoporosis and trochanteric bursitis."

"What the hell are you talkin' about?"

"You require medical assistance."

Yursfon hovers into an uncomfortably close position just beside Norman.

"The hell I do! Just help me up." Norman reaches trying to brace and prop himself up, leaning on the short robot, human hand to robot head. As he makes this attempt he feels a slight sting in his right side and looks down to find a strange metallic appendage extending from the robot with a hypodermic syringe at its tip, currently injecting fluids into Gramps' bloodstream.

Norman reacts violently, jumping back in the very same instant the robot retracts the needle extension back into its shell.

"What in the hell did you just do to me?!"

Norman quickly returns to his feet and takes a position that will allow him to either attack or flee in a moment's notice. He realizes, in the very same instant, that too long has it been since he was able to move and take such a stance without shooting pain being the common, overpowering result.

He currently feels no such pain, whatsoever.

"I've administered medical treatment. You've been injected with a collection of antibiotics, temporary adrenal stimulations, naproxen sodium, calcium, vitamin D, calcitonin, monoclonal antibodies, and arcalcictamox tissue reparation supplement."

"And that means what?"

"I have administered a minor stimulant and pain medications to temporary alleviate discomfort while the medications propagate. After the temporary stimulants subside in four hours, the pain you were experiencing should not return, as your osteoporosis and bursitis have both been treated."

"So, no more hip pain?"

Norman bends forward and backward in few short movements testing his newfound flexibility.

"'No more hip pain' due to treatable conditions, however, I cannot guarantee any relief from discomfort caused by conditions acquired at a later period."

"Fair 'nough, just s'long as I can walk."

The unlikely pair proceed once more with Norman following close behind the now fair-paced and obstacle-conscious assistance android. Stopping at what Norman recognizes to be a door, or, at least, the only feature he's seen for some time that even remotely resembles a door, albeit somewhat damaged with metal decay, he waits eagerly for the robot to open the exit and allow him to depart the disconsolate surroundings.

The small automated figure performs several hurried movements, and bobs its head up and down scanning over the door in an apparently frantic manner.

Oh dear! I shall be too late! Gramps thinks, recalling the rabbit leading Alice down the rabbit hole.

"Unfortunately, I seem to be encountering some technical difficulties. The storage access is simply not responding and I am incapable of identifying the cause of its current erroneous state."

"And what's all that mean?" Norman sighs, having predicted that his exit would, of course, come with some mass of difficulty.

"The door will not open, I'm afraid." Yursfon portrays a frantic vocal pattern matching the apparent faltering of confidence displayed in his movements.

"Bullshit. I'm getting out of this damn room, one way or another,"

Deciding to test his newly acquired freedom of movement, Norman swiftly kicks the bottom section of the solid metal door then responds to the resulting foot pain;

"Son of a bitch!"

"I recommend refraining from physically assaulting the access as it may cause further damage to both you and the access." Yursfon spins around to face Norman.

"Well, what the hell're we gonna do now?"

"I can remove the door from the frame with my internal emergency cutting torch, however, I will need to first request permission from technical administration as this will result in considerable damage to the access and they will need to determine if the financial loss in the resulting repair is warranted by such an operation. Their response may require twenty-four to forty-eight hours."

"Just do it. Cut the damn door, and get the permission later. This whole place looks like hell, they're gonna need to spend money fixing the door and probably everything else in here anyways."

"I am afraid I cannot proceed without proper instruction from technical administration."

"Listen, you talking toolbox, open the door, or I'm going to smash you open with a crate and rip the cutting torch out of you."

"This would not serve you in any meaningful way, *Gramps*, as the torch would no longer function."

Norman can almost detect a certain snideness accompanying the robot's remark.

"I might just do it anyways. Like I need a flying lunchbox following me around talking my damn ear off" Norman walks slowly over to a small crate and leans over to grasp it.

In response, Yursfon protracts his internal cutting torch and quickly hovers in a rectangular pattern around the frame. Within a few short seconds the door falls outward and smashes unto a red-orange desert floor blasting dust in nearly all directions.

Gramps stands up and turns to the small floating figure;

"Not a very smart robot are you? I was bluffing. I can't even lift that crate. Thing weighs a ton."

"I dispatched an expedited emergency request and received technical administrative permission."

"Sure ya did."

He did.

■ 12:41PM MARCH 2ND 3145

Sitting in a strange crescent-moon shaped seat floating a couple of feet above solid magnetic flooring, a young but decidedly large *Prictex Premium^ebr* technical administrative assistant, Yaundxe, stares blankly at the projected operational display windows as he does eight hours every day, six days a week. An emergency expedited permission request invades the bottom left corner of one of these windows and flashes, begging for his attention. Noting that it originates from Prictex Premium^ebr Energy and Travel Service Center three, thirty-four, alpha storage unit fourteen, Yaundxe is immediately irritated.

In his native Edirthaimic tongue, he turns to a fellow, slightly elder, yet considerably smaller technical administrative assistant and says, "Hey Stilv, look at this. It's that stupid Y-R-S, F-N forty-two sending another request. I don't know how much time I've wasted replying to this idiotic android. *Center three, thirty-four has been decommissioned and is no longer being supported.* Why can't we just deactivate these worthless models?"

"Who knows? It's policy. My guess, those models don't expend much energy, and those old storage units contain parts no longer being manufactured. And the Y-R-S, F-N models are the only ones still maintaining that old inventory. I guess they keep them active in the off-chance that we'll need old product."

"That's stupid." Yaundxe swivels in his chair.

"Yeah, pretty much. But, whatever, who cares. Log back into *Ixeshtar: Dungeon Frontiers* I need your *Level Sixteen Blaze Gun of Dalthuras* to finish this quest."

"Well, what should I tell this moronic unit? He wants to cut open the access door."

"What? Why?"

"I don't know. He doesn't really say. He says his continuing to function is dependent upon opening the access."

"What's that supposed to mean? Whatever, just say yes, otherwise, he'll probably just keep asking and I need that gun, now, moron."

"You're the moron, still at level twenty—Fine. *Proceed Y-R-S, F-N forty-two, the mighty level eighty-four technical administrative assistant, Yaundxe grants thee permission.*"

The young Edirthaimite chuckles as he enters his reply with a few quick seven-fingered hand gestures applied to a projected holographic control panel.

■ 12:47PM MARCH 2ND 3145

"Good God! Where'n the hell are we?"

Gramps stands just outside of the newly opened storage unit facing a completely alien red desert, set against dark, deformed and malicious looking mesas with green haze shifting along the horizon. He allows his eyes to follow one of many large and rapidly swirling swarms, and though he cannot make out clear shapes, it is clear that whatever living beings are forming these swarms, they are unlike anything he's ever seen in Arizona. The general dry heat, however, feels familiar.

"We are currently located at the Prictex Premium[ebr] Energy and Travel Service Center three, thirty-four Alpha Storage Unit Facilities, in the eastern, Ygrahd sector of the Braheliac continent, planet Edirthaimes. The nearest city is Vyrxhon Subsec two-hundred seventeen point zero one kilometers northeast, the nearest metropolitan is Eyridhaeus, four hundred twenty-five point fifty-six kilometers south. Do you require further information regarding our location?"

Yursfon gently progresses just beyond Gramps, stops, tilts and rotates his head as if to gesture the locations of the cities.

"Planet...ee-door-thame? I don't know how much more of this crap I can take."

IN RUINS (DIGITAL DAMES)

■ DATE AND TIME IN QUESTION

Rain burdened with acid from the atmosphere, falls in a symphony of percussive sounds as it strikes metal, asphalt and concrete with the shifts of the wind and clouds conducting each raucous movement in random rises and falls. The roof of a steel awning rife with decay and metal fatigue, rings and peels as the battery of drops cascade along its surface. Eddie's body lie dry, face-down beneath the steel ceiling seemingly unaware of the resonant assault occurring around him until the rainfall grows stronger, and reaches near-deafening tones. Silently, he rolls over unto his back and stares up at the battered steel surface sheltering him from the rain.

Eddie shivers lightly and sits up briefly surveying the immediate surroundings he can observe in the expanse just before the visibility wanes and distorts with the rain.

"Well...we've left Bowling."

With this thought he darts his head back and forth searching for the two who'd ventured with him and, again, can see very little beyond the excessive rainfall.

Finding a bench caked with grey dust, Eddie clears a small area and sits deciding to wait out the rain, not daring to venture beyond the shelter of the awning in what looks like a harsh and potentially hazardous rainfall. Across from the rows of benches Eddie spots blinking terminal screens lined up beside one another like phone stations. All but one displays an error message proclaiming deactivated service.

Eddie decides to use, or at least try to use, the only apparently operational terminal, but has limited experience with any electronics beyond the calculator, or cash register.

He figures he'll draw from the knowledge acquired during those few times he'd used the *Commodore 64* in the Bowling library. Unfortunately this knowledge only includes the ability to use the most basic form of BASIC, the word processor *SpeedScript,* and *Space Taxi;* a game at which he was admittedly unskilled.

Up close and personal with the terminal, Eddie is shocked with what he sees, being accustomed to large heavy monitors with bulky keyboards, he sees only a simple metal pole with a concave section near the top, surrounding a hole projecting minimalist but crisp graphic visuals in a rounded rectangular shape suspended in midair just beyond the poles surface. Strictly out of dumbfounded curiosity, Eddie leans over and makes an attempt to peer into the hole as if this will somehow reveal the unbelievable technology producing the fantastic illusions. Instead, a bright light flashes, temporarily blinding his right eye.

A feminine voice with a sweet and soothing tone that Eddie assumes must be emitting from the metal column, states with an accompanied textual display;

"I'm sorry; I cannot identify you as a citizen. This terminal's services are citizen use only. You may repeat the retinal scan if you feel there has been an error. If you require assistance, please select the option on display or simply ask for help."

The translucent screen projects an entirely new design presenting, with mostly red flashing letters and graphics, an alarming and somehow ominous tone. The two highlighted options seem to demand a response as the act of being identified as a citizen is critical. Eddie decides it best to avoid further contact with the terminal.

"Please repeat the retinal scanning process or request assistance."

The initially friendly voice is now demanding and seems prepared to begin issuing threats. Eddie isn't accustomed to responding to demands made by speaking posts and decides his efforts would be better served braving the rain.

"At least it's calmed down some."

Eddie looks out beyond the terminals and finds a disparaging sight just beyond him. Metal and concrete buildings in various states of decay, rise above masses of rubble and refuse, surrounding a street of disrepair. With no sense of familiarity in his surroundings, Eddie believes his only reasonable option is to follow the road before him.

Eddie considers calling out some familiar names in hopes that he isn't the only wayward wanderer to have arrived in the dank remains of what must have once been a sprawling metropolis, but cannot decide if he wants to bring attention to himself when he has no idea who or what may be dwelling within the obscured, foreboding ruins.

"TIM...JILL...RONNIE!"

And to a lesser extent, in a lower voice;

"MIKE!"

Eddie throws caution with voice into the wind and sincerely hopes he doesn't stir something he can't fend against or at least outrun.

"EDDIE! Fuckin' hell! S'that you?" It's Mike. Nowhere near Eddie's first choice for a companion in a deserted island situation, but he figures it fits the trend of a worst-case scenario.

Eddie darts his head around and begins scanning the general direction from which Mike's voice seems to have emanated. He spots the silhouette of his larger-than-life companion, standing beneath the dilapidated remains of what resembles a loading bay for one of the taller buildings in the immediate area.

Waving his hands furiously in an attempt to draw the attention of the already aware, Mike shouts;

"Get over here, out of the rain. That shit's hazardous."

Eddie quickly jogs through the rain; crossing cracked pavement, dissolving concrete and softening steel until finally passing through the large bay doorway. He hunches over to catch his breath, wondering why his lungs have tightened so much in response to what seemed to be only a few hurried steps.

Mike pats his back;

"Tell me about it, I feel like I've run a marathon or somethin'. And this air reeks fierce."

Eddie begins to notice the strange and caustic odor as it becomes intensified only after stepping out of the rain; he isn't sure what to make of it. Still hunched down, he notices his arms have become bright red and now can feel the irritation caused by the drops of corrupted water pelting his exposed limbs. Lifting his arm to his nose in an apish manner he is made aware that his skin is secreting the offensive stench.

"You and me both Eddie. We're gonna smell like this shit for days. I don't know what the hell kind of rain that is. Could strip the paint off a car. It feels like it's gonna strip my damned skin off too."

"Where in the hell are we?" Eddie stands and tries to wring his shirt dry, twisting the light fabric in various places.

"I dunno. Looks like a loading bay for a mall or somethin'. Reminds me of that one movie, you know, where they're all stuck in that mall with the fuckin' zombies."

Looking around Mike surveys the severely decayed remains of storage shelves, wood shipping pallets, and two small machines that closely resemble forklifts.

It's totally picked clean in here. He internally remarks after noticing the surprising absence of any of the usual products and items that should typically line the shelves.

"Don't say that Mike. After what we just went through, the walking undead probably isn't far off. Shit, it even looks like someone's been holed up in here, and all of the stock here's been picked over."

Gesturing to a corner of the large room where a box and an old sleeping bag could be seen perched under a short overhang that likely used to be a part of another floor above, Eddie supports his argument.

"Yeah, this building's torn to shit. It doesn't look right neither, I mean, it sure as hell ain't like any building I've seen in Bowling. Fucking walls look like melted plastic or some shit."

Michael walks briefly through the bay minding to keep his face shielded from the rain when not under the bits of ceiling still available.

"Whoa! What the..."

Michael's voice trails off as he disappears behind a series of shelves in the distance.

"Michael! Where the hell'd you go?"

Eddie waits a few moments, hoping for a quick reply from his friend.

No response.

"Damn it, Mikey." Towards the back of the bay, glancing quickly from left to right peering through shelving units as he passes by, Eddie leads his short solo excursion in search of Mike.

Michael was right. There seems to be a certain ambiguity to the shape and design of everything Eddie surveys, even beyond the appearance of fire damage and corrosion.

For one thing, Eddie thinks, *there's no rust. Everything looks metallic but nothing in here is rusted.*

With everything conveying the appearance of significant age and corrosion, the lack of rust strikes Eddie. Though clearly not metal, plastic isn't quite accurate either, rather, it looks to be some synthetic compound amalgamating the properties of multiple firm materials. Certainly too expensive and discerningly developed a material to be featured in his rustic hometown.

Scanning the walls, he walks and wonders at the paneled shapes and grooves which meet almost seamlessly with the translucent flooring.

Eddie suddenly notices the silence with Mike's absence. The building gives no audible response to its being struck violently with rain. He finds it unsettling, to say the least. Eddie had watched many sci-fi movies growing up and enjoyed none more so than those tempered in the fires of horror and suspense, of these he'd seen enough to draw numerous references. He concludes that if he finds himself to be somewhere in the future, one crawling with the unnamable and mutated remnants of man, one or two of those filmmakers could sleep soundly knowing they were, in fact, ahead of their time, at least in terms of set design.

Spotting a large shipping container featuring some sleek, impenetrable design, Eddie notices bright blue light emitting from an opening at its back. He feels his skin rise and excite in goose bumps as his mind relentlessly replays shocking scenes from childhood films. He thinks to himself, *don't go in there you stupid idiot*. Eddie manages to make himself smile with the ludicrous thought that something with long, glistening claws coated with bits of a previous prey's flesh and rows of razor-like teeth dripping with the lifeblood of thousands of poor unsuspecting fools is waiting to tear him asunder and devour his remains.

Movement obstructs the light and defines a shifting shape of something large and lumbering inhabiting the container.

Eddie's smile fades.

It may be best not to proceed; it may be absurd to allow curiosity to overcome the natural, instinctual flight response which demands a retreat from possible danger.

But what the hell else am I gonna do?

Approaching cautiously, Eddie tries to ease his fear yelling loudly;

"Michael, s'that you?! Where the hell are you?!"

Begrudgingly Eddie leans around the corner of the container and peers through the lighted opening. For a moment, he is taken aback, and his mind pauses as it struggles to best define the sight his eyes are currently translating, but it fails and admits that it cannot quite fathom what Eddie beholds.

Michael stands before several brightly-lit cases, containing small platforms that project incredible life-size, and realistically animated, three-dimensional and oft dancing figures, each appearing with minor variations leaving them otherwise identical to their recently missing friend, Veronica.

SOUND CHECK (RADIO CURES)

"What the hell? Gramps? Still alive in thirty-one, forty-seven, that's gotta be a record."

Shaking his head Tim sighs in befuddlement.

"So what's this supposed to mean?"

He looks down to Pete, who has no answers but understands he needs none with the rhetorical nature of the question. He offers up a questioning yelp just the same, if only to share the response to the perplexing find.

Tim presses his finger into a select area of the display; a sort of button groove surrounding a small image resembling an open lock. The display changes to a prompt requesting Norman's twelve digit numerical locker pin.

"What's your birthdate Pete?"

Tim, again, peers down at the still perplexed dog.

"We've got all the time in whatever shitty world this is, but I'm not gonna spend half of it trying to figure out some fuckin' locker code."

Tim figures that before pursuing some other likely aimless task he may as well try a few numbers before giving up.

"I don't know Pete, how 'bout mine and Eddie's birthdates. Eddie's is..."

After a brief moment spent in mental search Tim recalls the date and enters one, twenty-three, fifty-nine followed by his ten, nine, sixty-three.

"Shit that's not enough numbers."

He makes a second attempt adding zeroes before the single digits and with that ,the display responds executing a prerecorded clicking sound and a short animation of a lock unlocking.

"No shit, Gramps? Guess you're not the favorite, Pete."

Looking to the dog with a smirk; for a moment Tim's nearly certain he hears Pete growl.

He does, but for an altogether unrelated reason. In the distance a faint sound of movement, flight of some kind, with a distinction produced by what must be a massive object, or possibly subject, can be heard. By Pete's estimate, it must be roughly thirty-seven and one-third miles away, moving slowly and even stopping on occasion as if in the process of searching for something. He's never been too adept at judging the exact size of things moving through the air, based merely on sound, but if pressed to make an assumption, Pete would guess the yet unidentified flying subject's weight to be roughly three tons.

If the subject's movement were to continue in their direction at its current perceived rate, it should be in view within the hour. At which point, Pete premeditates, he will ensure Tim's attention is suitably redirected. For now his mind is thoroughly encompassed by curiosity in regards to the contents of the locker Tim just opened.

Tim peers into the strange compartment divided into three shelving units, each with its own lighted paneling. Upon the first shelf sits a portion of a dog collar with the large imprint of the name 'Pete' on one of its metal tags. With this are three spent shotgun shells atop a small but incredibly detailed painting of a familiar dog sitting beside his familiar elderly companion.

The second shelf is mostly vacant, save for a small, flat, rectangular black object with three blinking lights on the bottom lip of the objects surface. Sitting beside this, is a white piece of some type of shell that appears to have been charred or burned along one side.

The third shelf contains a pair of worn jeans, a flannel shirt, and some old discolored socks, all matching the clothes Gramps had been wearing when Tim had last seen him. Pete anxiously sniffs and nudges his nose through the clothing pile collecting, analyzing and finding some minor comfort in the strong familiar scents they still secrete.

Tim retrieves the collar, ties the break, and affixes it around Pete's neck, as he continues to inhale the memories. He places the folded up painting in his back pocket with his wallet, and with no idea as to what he is actually acquiring, Tim reaches into the locker one final time to take the strange blinking device.

Pete backs quickly out of the locker and begins growling furiously before escalating into a barking fit. He runs to Tim, jumps on his leg and runs back to the door. This series of movements is repeated three times before Tim finishes stuffing his pockets and closes the locker.

"Alright Pete. What the hell is it now?"

Only seconds after this question, Tim is made to realize he needs no reply. He hears, and what's more, through the wall in the not so great and moonlit distance, he sees the disturbance as well.

■ 10:39PM

An object, still unidentified and flying, at a height of just over twenty feet above the ground, approaches at a speed slightly quicker than Pete's estimate.

"What the fuck is that?!"

Tim loudly issues the currently unanswerable question.

The massive flying vehicle quickly comes into view and dominates the right segment of Tim's view of the horizon with a gunmetal grey and silver hued body lightly reflecting the browns, reds and greens of the landscape. Tim surmises that in lesser light it would probably escape visibility.

Bright lime-green light beams abruptly from within a thin center crevice that appears to circumference the entire vehicle as it slows to a stop. Blasting out in all directions ,the beams crawl and climb along the landscape far beyond any perceptible realm, coating what must be an immense radius with an aura of green, grid-like formations. In an instant, the light retreats back into the center of the vehicle which itself ceases to exist in any visible dimension.

It's disappeared.

Pete continues to bark, as though visually non-existent; he knows from the almost inaudible drone of the now unmoving object, it is still present. Waiting. Betraying its own attempt at illusion with interior engine movement that could only be considered silent to all but the most discerning and perceptive of creatures. Pete's ears perk and rotate, tuning and receiving every physical change the vehicle makes, however miniscule.

"You still hear it Pete? Good, let's get the fuck out of here. You keep barking until we're nowhere near that thing. Whatever it is."

Using the control panel he's now become familiar with, Tim exits the warehouse through the large illusionary door with Pete following close behind.

Now running, Tim and Pete quickly leave the building behind and traverse clumsily along the barren landscape stretching beyond one side of the station kicking monazite, cobalt and iron oxide laden dust in large thickets behind them. Tim had considered being conspicuous but decided speed would be of greater use, and *who knows*, he thinks, *they might not care that we're here*. A few childhood memories of being caught breaking-and-entering lead him to believe otherwise.

The engine noise becomes audible, now even to Tim, who fears breaking stride, even slightly to allow a brief shoulder glance to see how close behind the vehicle is chasing, if it *is* chasing, or if it's decided to reveal itself.

The vast terrain begins descending as Tim's pocketed radio suddenly issues familiar static groans. The two have no intention of slowing even as the radio sounds grow more intense, almost defeating Pete's boisterous bark. The engine noise grows too behind them, and all three sounds converge if only to force Tim's pulse into unhealthy rhythms just before he stops cold in his tracks with Pete following suit beside him.

Only a foot beyond the two would-be escapists drops a cliff three-hundred feet down into a low ground that is coated for miles of barely visible area with black. Like an ocean of pure violence, the expansive dark material cascades and abrades into itself with crashing waves of hooked, jagged, and genuinely uninviting liquid forms.

Tim decides finally, to turn around and face the engine-pumping beast that seems to give chase behind him. Pete, no longer barking, does the same and stands in silence mentally cycling through dozens of imaginary scenarios proposing the moments soon to come.

They face a floating vehicular machine, roughly eighty feet wide, seventy feet tall, and two hundred feet long by Tim's best estimates. Ninety-three feet wide, eighty-one feet, two inches tall, and two-hundred, twenty-seven feet long by Pete's. Whatever the exact size may be, they would both agree; it is very large.

Pete considers that for such a mass, the engine is remarkably quiet and efficient, and stands impressed in many more ways than he would've initially surmised. He finds the situation both terrifying and fascinating with either response competing for the highest mental favor. Tim, on the other hand, is without question, terrified. Being mere moments away from losing complete control of urinary functions, he finds nothing particularly fascinating at current.

Throughout the years of his youth, Tim had been arrested only once, at fifteen, after using some bricks and a cinder block to obliterate several windows in the west wing of the small

Bowling High School late one night in the summer. He recalls this moment as he stands with fear quaking through his body and a voice blasts loudly from somewhere around the vehicle accompanied by a bright light emitted with equal intensity upon his face and body. Only then, it was an officer exiting a squad car with a flash light beaming upon him and demanding he drop the brick and raise his hands. He has no idea what demands the occupants of the vehicle before him are issuing, but he responds now, as he did then, and throws up his arms, waiting with quiet dread for whatever is to ensue.

Nothing happens; instead the alien shouting persists and Pete responds with more barking. The radio never once cuts the steady stream of static and the engine is still overt in its audibility. Tim finds that he cannot stand much more and decides to join in the noisy exchanges.

He drops his hands to his sides in fists and shouts;
"SHUT THE FUCK UP!"

Pete stops, the shouting stops, and the engine silences as the vehicle appears to enter an idle state.

The radio however, continues. Tim turns back to face the sea of darkness and angrily throws the relentless radio over the cliff.

Silence.

Until Pete barks.

Tim turns around once more and watches as six gargantuan and apish, crab-like creatures file out in a double line formation from an opening in the side of the vehicle.

Still watching in terror, Tim observes the creatures as they quickly scuttle out of the machine towards him. Each is supported by four large appendages resembling crab legs. In addition to these legs, there are two large armored arms, ending with three claws positioned with two of the claws opposing the third jutting from a hand structured with a slight similarity to that of a primate. These are attached to an ant-like abdomen and thorax which sits upright atop the legs. Six eyes form a V-formation in the center of their unusually small and rigid heads, just above two protruding mandibles which appear as much smaller replicas of the crab-like legs. Tucked just beneath these chelicerae are five independently flailing tentacles which appear to be coated in wispy, viscous saliva. Each carries an apparatus in both hands that could only be likened to a gun.

A more exact description of the weapon each of these unidentified creatures possess would be particle emitting plasma projectile eruption rifle, or PEPPER, powered by Maeloid, a source of energy only found in trace quantities on Earth and massive quantities on Edirthaimes, which fires plasma in short, rapid and exceedingly concentrated bursts. The resulting wound found on those unlucky enough to be on the receiving end of this particular form of weaponry, is aptly known as the pepper burn, and is considered by all accounts, a ghastly sight.

The group of unpleasant-looking beings stop just short of Tim and one begins to shout demands in plain English;

"WHAT DID YOU JUST THROW? GET DOWN ON THE GROUND! ARMS OUT, AWAY FROM YOUR SIDES. DO IT NOW! NOW!"

With this last 'now' the shouting being thrusts its weapon forward and down with the barrel tip just inches away from touching Tim's recoiling forehead.

Tim, wisely follows the order and lies stomach down on the ground with his arms stretched out, away from his sides.

The creature repeats; "WHAT DID YOU JUST THROW?"

"I—uh...It was just a radio. It was making too much noise." Tim replies nervously.

"A WHAT."

"A radio, damnit!"

Tim's initial fear subsides, once again replaced with aggravation.

The apparent leader turns to the creature to its right and clicks out an unidentifiable question;

"Klarrock tockclick addonick larkick radio, eckstclick?"

The right-hand being responds with a shrug and a muttered;

"Kloanoaclick."

"What the fuck is this?"

Tim utters the few words and sighs, blowing away dust from the ground.

"SHUT UP!"

The creature shouts and leans in further with its gun aimed appropriately at Tim's head.

Tim rocks his head slightly along his chin in desperation.

"What is a radio?"

The creature, though no longer shouting, is clearly stern.

"It's just something that...plays music and crap."

Tim blows more dirt into the air before him in attempt to clear it away from his face. The creature snarls lightly, pulls its gun in towards its face and takes aim at Tim's back.

Tim shudders and closes his eyes.

With a click of some unseen button on the side of the weapon a bright series of green lasers, similar to the lights from the vehicle, emit from a lens just below the barrel and quickly retract.

"Unusually high body mass for such a small frame. Primarily oxygen and carbon."

The leader looks up from the gun and peers to its right.

The lackey at the right responds;

"Human?"

Returning its attention to Tim the leader asks;

"Are you human?"

"No shit, I'm human. What the hell are you supposed to be and why the hell can I understand what you're saying? You look like a fuckin' crab-spider."

"SHUT UP!"

Again the barrel is focused towards Tim's head.

"Oral-Linquistulators translate speech matching the speech patterns to whatever being is targeted. I am Xuergass Stracbagf. Now, tell me what business you have here."

"I don't even know where the hell I am. I don't know how I got here, and I don't know what the fuck's going on. How 'bout you Pete? I cover everything?"

Tim turns his head to see the dog, which has remained silent for the entire conversation.

Pete rifles quickly through every piece of information collected and can only postulate that they are not in Bowling, they are not on planet Earth, it is not nineteen-eighty-six, rather hundreds of years later, the black matter has somehow spirited them away, and they are currently being badgered by a species of a profoundly alien origin. Unfortunately, not one of these small pieces of insight could be applied to answer Tim's question with any comfortable certainty. He cocks his head slightly and whines as if to say; *Beats me.*

The monstrous quadruped turns its attention to Pete and continues;

"YOU! SPEAK! WHAT IS YOUR BUSINESS HERE? WHAT MATTER OF BEING ARE YOU?"

"He can't talk dipshit, he's a dog." Tim responds in Pete's stead.

"SHUT UP! IF YOU SPEAK OUT OF TURN ONCE MORE, YOU WILL BE EXECUTED."

Again, the leader turns to its right with another question for its evident second in command;

"Klarrock tockclick addonick larkick dog, eckstclick?"

And again, the right-hand creature responds with a shrug and a muttered;

"Kloanoaclick."

The leader then focuses its aim upon Pete and demands;

"SPEAK! I WILL NOT TOLERATE FURTHER INSOLENCE!"

Pete lowers his head, bears his teeth with a growl and barks.

Green lasers beam once more from the gun.

"Similar composition, a feral creature of some sort. Appears to lack linguistic capabilities. "

"No shit. DOGS...DON'T...TALK!"

Tim mocks the being in an attempt to spur things along, having grown weary of the proceedings.

In response, the creature snarls loudly throws its arms up and violently slams the back of its rifle into Tim's skull.

"Shut up."

DENIZENS (OF A STRANGE LAND)

Ronnie follows the rapid-paced Gnuella through intensely lit corridors and along street-side walkway ramps managing to navigate through various confusing redirections which seem to contradict the common order used along the routes, as indicated by the bright motioning arrows and guidelines polluting the space, walls, and flooring around them. The paths and streets become sparse, dim and clearly less travelled as they progress descending to the surface levels of the city.

Stopping, Ronnie looks before her after the large man guiding her through the labyrinthine city.

"Alright! I was stupid to follow you without asking this, I guess all of those blinding lights and obnoxious noises have that effect on people. But, where the hell are you taking me... *New-Ella*?"

Ronnie purposely exaggerates the pronunciation of her new-found guide's name.

"Heh. I've been waiting for that question cheello. Ponset, I's baftred you dockssed a guf like me. Delphines ugeses only leeds on breddy bades. And I ain't no bade of no kind."

Gnuella rests his arm upon Ronnie's shoulder and dons effeminate light tones and matching fluttering facial expressions as his eyes cautiously follow a uniformed and armed man mechanically patrolling along a surface street just beyond them.

After the man is out of sight, Gnuella removes his arm from Ronnie's shoulder, smiles lightly and leans in to quietly repeat himself;

"I've been waiting for that question. I'm surprised you even followed a guy like me. An attractive woman like you typically wouldn't spare words for men who are not equally pretty, feminine or even boyish. And I would never be considered pretty in any respect—Just in case you were wondering what I said."

Gnuella steps back and winks. He then bows his head slightly and gestures Ronnie to carry on down the alley they now face.

"Okay, first off, that's really creepy. I followed you because you made it sound like I didn't have much of a choice. When you say you're surprised I came along with you, it makes me think you're full of shit. And I warn you, I've put guys in hospitals for thinking they can pull somethin' on me."

Veronica becomes almost combative in her stance and with some sharp pointing indicates her readiness to become very aggressive.

Gnuella attempts to interject;

"I didn't—" and is interrupted.

"Second, I really need you stop talking like you're some homeboy airhead, and tell me where the hell we're going."

Gnuella leans in again.

"Okay. Calm down and try to keep quiet. I'm sorry for the strange behavior, but in this society; this language, this attire, and these mannerisms are more than common. You're not the only one who hates it, I once spoke that way to my father and he struck me in the jaw. But here, anything outside of the common raises suspicion...suspicion is a very bad thing. You may not have noticed the man patrolling along the street a second ago, but that was an associate, an A-M-A, and that he's even allowed himself to be visible is disconcerting. It means they find you...us, suspicious, and they are clearly watching us and with enough severity they've the volition of making us aware."

"My grandfather once said '*in the city the sore thumbs don't just stick out, they're cut off!*'. And in so many words, that's the best way I can justify this façade."

Pausing briefly Gnuella directs Ronnie to continue following him down the alley, she does so, but questions her own obedience.

After three additional turns through the paths between the monolithic skyscrapers and a short traversal through the narrowest of the passages Ronnie has encountered in the city, or ascosite, of Domaves.

Gnuella continues;

"It means we need to move quickly, we're heading to a town about two-hundred and fifteen kilometers north of here...my hometown, of the unreqs, Tierka Avengladors. It will be easier to gather our thoughts and we'll need my brother's help in finding information regarding your friend, among other things. He's sort an information expert, he keeps tabs on just about every piece of news that flows through this or any other city."

Gnuella stops just beside a large metal bin standing against a similarly metallic wall belonging to one of the many towering buildings. He points forward and nods to Ronnie. She looks to the end of the alley as directed and sees a great metal wall which stretches far into the sky beyond view with a small but solid door at the base being the only variation in the slick, constant and overwhelming barrier.

"That's the ascosite gate, and don't let it's unassuming subtlety fool you. It's heavily fortified, and it is one of only four exits out of this ascosite. Only associates have the ability to use it. Those of the ascosite are not meant to leave."

Gnuella leaves Ronnie with a grim tone and begins to push the bin along the wall belonging to one of the cloud piercing surface structures. Ronnie assumes the weight of the metal container must be immense, as the large-bodied and large-armed Gnuella doesn't appear as if he would have much trouble lifting a car let alone some garbage bin, or whatever it may be.

"Would you mind helping me push this disposal unit?"

Gnuella looks back to Veronica who is once again staring at the city wall and gate.

"Sorry...I don't know why I'm even going along with this; I just need to find Tim. But, he probably wouldn't be caught dead in this city, and something tells me that anything that gets me out of here is a good thing."

The two cooperatively move the disproportionately heavy waste unit to reveal a slender slot, at the base of the structure, which appears to lead below the surface of the building and city. To where, Ronnie can only imagine. Gnuella leans down and points into the opening. Ronnie, too, leans down and peers in. The area is dark and all that can be seen is a marking on a wall somewhere below. Created in that same luminescent paint, the marking appears to bear the shape of a large bird.

An ostrich? What the hell is that supposed to mean?

Ronnie turns to Gnuella as if to pose the question telepathically.

He responds, "Well cheello, you ready to leave this place behind? Ladies first."

Gnuella gestures to the opening and bows.

She nods with the answer '*yes*' but vocalizes a caveat;

"I'll go, but I can't see anything."

"'*The Avengladors never fear the dark, as it is all we have to keep us safe.*' My father would say this to me when I was young and having trouble sleeping on particularly dark nights. I'll follow, right after you, and once we pull the waste unit behind us and seal the opening I'll activate the light—I don't mean to worry you, but we have already spent far too much time here, we need to move now before the A-M-A turns an associates eyes to this otherwise unmonitored alley."

Ronnie climbs through the narrow gap and allows her body to drop, hoping she meets the invisible ground sooner rather than later. Too soon, the floor of the room must only be five feet from the ceiling forcing her to crouch slightly. She can only imagine how much the gargantuan cross-dresser following behind her will be forced to hunch over.

She turns to see him struggle briefly through and not so much drop, as simply place his large feet upon the floor. He hunches over in an almost ninety-degree position and grabs a small handle protruding from the back of the disposal container. Ronnie follows suit and assists the great, made-up man in pulling the unit over the gap.

Gnuella presses his hand into a section of his shirt on the left side of his chest and a solid circle of bright white forms around his fingers. Ronnie squints and turns her eyes away from an intense light now beaming from Gnuella's left breast and finds the room completely illuminated.

"See! Nothing to fear in this darkness. Just an abandoned underground transport tube station that became defunct around the twenty-one hundreds along with the entire city it serviced. And like countless ancient cities before this one they simply built over and forgot it, as if it never existed. Maybe one day they'll lead tours down here. Until then, it's Avenglador territory."

Gnuella points to the ostrich graffiti once more. He smiles at Ronnie;

"Feel free to look around, we won't need to rush at this depth, the A-M-A rarely steps foot into the underground city. It used to be patrolled by automated militarized units, but detectable intrusions, or attempts to leave without passing through the gates, became such a rarity after the advent of phenocuphiline, they deemed the underground patrol an unnecessary expense. Anymore it's just countless rats, bugs, snakes, and the occasional Avenglador. And right now, you look more the part than I."

Ronnie wasn't sure if this was meant as a complement, but if it implies Avengladors dress like normal people, she at least would be more comfortable wherever they were heading.

So she takes a brief look around the station as Gnuella uses a nearby window as a mirror to help remove the make-up caked upon his face.

"Fee-no-suh…" Ronnie attempts to pronounce the word and is interrupted with correction;

"Phenocuphiline, a greatly encouraged pharmaceutical distributed freely within the ascosites and sold at intentionally affordable rates to the unreqisitioned zones. It's psychoactive, calming, and ultimately sterilizes users of any desires not considered productive. '*Keeping the peace*' thus becomes affordable, efficient and painless."

Gnuella says this as if selling a product, but Ronnie can detect the ironic currents flowing with his words. He continues removing his disguise and carries on with his informative account;

"Most every citizen uses the drug. Many of those from the unreqs do as well, but slowly, the people of unreqs are beginning to realize their purpose."

"Okay…"

Ronnie commits most of the information to memory and considers its implications for a moment, but allows her mind to stray as she surveys her surroundings.

The station is clearly derelict, and shows little signs of use aside from the strange bird marking. Scattered around the room are some strange minimalist seats, most worn beyond use, broken remnants of small metallic pylons and bits and pieces from shattered terminal screens encompassing the walls. All point to technologies precursor to the surface city but likely still more advanced than anything ever found in Bowling. This sparks a question in Veronica's mind.

She decides to voice the thought, "You've been telling me about all of these things and answering my questions while I follow you around like I'm lost in the dark…and I'm stupidly trusting you. So—"

Ronnie turns to find a different man now facing her. Still wearing the same horrible clothes, the large man, completely free of make-up and the circular patch of hair, evidently a tou-pee, now stands before her with a natural coffee brown face and brown eyes which better coalesce the prominent mascu-line features he was previously attempting to hide. His now bald head features an intricate arrangement of blood-red tribal markings which stop and form fittingly just around the eyes. Though still clothed in style of the ascosite, Ronnie considers that his appearance has become far more bearable, if not more intimidating.

"You're wondering why I haven't questioned you more regarding your situation. My grandfather once told me that we should never assume our customs, our knowledge, our life-styles are definitive. The world is full of strangers from strange lands, and with them, entirely different cultures and ways of life. Naivety is a relative curse, and everyone bears it in their own way. I didn't ask because I didn't think it was my place, I only knew you were not from the city, and that it meant you would be in danger. This city thrives on naivety, and anything that introduces something new is not tolerated."

Gnuella speaks in his natural voice, deep and powerful but surging with undercurrents of wisdom and compassion.

"But I'll admit I'm curious. So, who's this Tim, is he from your small unrequisitioned town?"

"Yeah, Tim's...my boyfriend, should be fiancée, if he'd just figure that out already. And we're both from a tiny sun-dried old town...very far from here. If you'd ever seen it, you'd know there's not much more to say about it, and to be honest anything else I can add...would just lead to a long unbelievable story."

Ronnie sets up one of the broken seats upon some rubble and sits still facing Gnuella.

"Fair enough, I won't pry. That's my brother's specialty, not mine. His name is Tim too, by the way. Of course, it's short for Timmarbalo and judging by your reaction, I doubt that's your Tim's proper name."

Gnuella uses the light jest as an opportunity to reveal his natural smile.

Ronnie chuckles and returns the smile; "Nope, nothing so exotic, if that is exotic I mean. No offense. His name's Timmothy. He does spell it with two 'M's though, so it makes it a little less common."

"Timmarbalo would be exotic to the cities, but it's not a name unique to the unrequisitioned zones...most of them anyways. We really shouldn't linger too long, we're safe from the A-M-A, but if you're Tim is missing, it's probably best that we get to my Tim and begin the search as soon as possible."

"Besides, this is the home of the Obverts. They eat the children who venture into the underground."

Gnuella walks to a window within the remnants of a building they now occupy and peers out at the ruins of the mostly street-less city cankered with shattered transport tubes once used to rocket small vehicles from point-to-point at dangerously high velocities proving time and time again to be too dangerous to be useful, one of the many reasons this prototypical city failed and now only serves as a foundation for a far more successful, if not more daunting, metropolis.

"What the hell is that? You said there's nothing to fear down here. Just an old ruined city."

Breaking her stance Ronnie walks to the window to share the view.

"There isn't. It's just an old folk tale parents tell their children to keep them out of the underground. It's strange, really, everyone in the unrequisitioned zones knows about the underground but everyone in the ascosite is completely oblivious to its existence, I'm not sure many of the A-M-A associates know about it."

Gnuella turns around and stares at the rubble on the floor as if deep in though. He begins walking again with Ronnie following close behind. They climb down a ramp formed through years of falling metal, concrete and stone-work and in their deep descent find the street level of the underground city. Ronnie looks skyward in an attempt to perceive the ceiling. Gnuella takes notice and repositions himself to shift the light upward.

The two have distanced themselves nearly two-hundred meters from the once uncomfortably close ceiling. Ronnie continues to gaze through the dimly lit beyond at the metal and stone sky before observing all that can be seen with the details lost in the expanse, she turns to Gnuella and the two continue advancing through the city as he begins a lengthy orchestration of words.

"There's even a well-known poem from one of the town's out in the unreq's. It's written after an old tale about one of the underground cities; Obvert. It's called *The Subculture*:

In the dire setting of vast defunct transport tubes
Those once connecting the largest of metropolitans,
A new society is born of abandoned remnants.
A forever perverted wasteland of the forgotten,
A subvert culture for the corrupted prototypes
Prototypes of the modern man.

In this decaying land of collected atrocities,
Procreation is a means to provide sustenance.
Death is an instrument of the living
Operated so often it holds no significance
No more than those sites where the corpses are left,
Those sites where the discarded are left to putrefy.

Ideals form as besmirched mockeries,
That of the wreckage forebears.
There are no gods and there is no reason.
With the moment at hand as the definitive.
No thoughts are spared for the past,
No thoughts are given to the future.

Any unity capable of burgeoning,
Is hindered by the ultimate narcissism.
It is implied by the need for survival,
But it is at best, as are all things,
All things ever guaranteed;
Are guaranteed only a fleeting life.

As life itself is stripped of all luxuries,
Stripped of necessities and dignities,
Those only inherit to the civilized;
It is reduced to a mere struggle,
A survival contending with the only absolute,
An absolute of adversity.

This world of the condemned,
It knows only one truth;
That age is the only measure of fortune.
The elders are kings.
Those with the necessary strength,
The cunning, endurance, and constitution.
They are the only individuals able, enabled.
Enabled through the sparse benefit of experience.

But even these lords of scavenge are bastardized,
Receiving only the begrudged respect,
Encumbered with fear and caution,
From those others born into this savage.
This world of exaggerated lust, and gluttony.
This land of malice.

While the meek, the pure, and the feeble,
They are discarded by the abandoned,
And they turn to refuse by the wayside.

Once they'd fed the strong,
Strong though barely living.
They, ironically fortunate.

It knows only one name, this land.
A name who's meaning,
Has been long lost,
Lost to the contaminated dust.
A name whispered lightly in the rubble,
They call it Obvert.

"That's a poem? That's terrible. They don't tell that to kids do they? Telling them that some people have kids so they can eat them, how would children even understand that?"

Ronnie now looks upon her surroundings with greater observation, caution and distinct disgust.

"Of course not, it's a more contemporary composition. Sort of a modern psalm, it's supposed to draw parallels to the ascosites, mocking their secular nature. It's merely based around the children's folk tale."

Gnuella stops walking and surveys the buried world around them once more before adding;

"I have heard it performed in song, though, with a somehow upbeat rhythm. It's actually one of my favorites; I guess that's why I have it memorized. Anyway the eating people part is the least shocking, at least in the city."

"What!?"

"Well, not quite to the dramatized extent of the poem, but, in the city, it's not uncommon to extract the otherwise scarce protein compounds and complex carbohydrates from the recently deceased. In fact, the meat from the dead is more desirable than most other meats developed using artificial cell structures."

Gnuella treats the subject with a lack of gravity Ronnie finds deeply disturbing.

"Good lord! That's insane. *You* don't eat that shit do you?"

Though concerned Ronnie considers for a moment that his grandfather's words should apply, she's in a strange world with a complete stranger, and she has no concept of what's taboo or commonplace.

But eating people is groddy, especially if there are options. Any options.

"No, out in the unreq's, it's mostly wild boar and coyote. I prefer boar—Here, stick closely now. The city opens up greatly here and it can be easy to lose your way. The Avengladors leave coded tracks that can be detected and decoded with one of these," Gnuella retrieves from a thin slot in his shirt, a small rectangular frame with a transparent center and holds it up over the wall marked with the Avengladors insignia.

"Sure...let's go."

Ronnie, having followed Gnuella out of the station and down into the crumbled city at a short distance, trying to keep within his light, now stands close behind Gnuella and watches over his shoulder as the thin framed screen in his hands makes strange three-dimensional shapes that apparently direct where to proceed.

"So, not everybody around here's a total freak after all. Here, it turns out Avenglador's only wear make-up to fit in with the city folk, *why that's a trend, I'm sure, makes no sense.* And they can actually use normal English, and they don't eat people."

"For the most part, this is true. But, my family is actually one of few in the western unreqs still speaking English outside of the cities. Most speak a language native to the western zones, *Espramutte.*"

Gnuella emphasizes the word with exaggerated pronunciation. To Ronnie it sounds something like 'ess-praw-moot.'

She continues watching the screen as they walk slowly and carefully through broken relics and rubble. Gnuella notices her attempt at deciphering the images on the screen.

"We've coated several of the walls with adherents that project ultra-violet lights in the form of binary messages written in a deconstructed code based around complex algorithms that must be decrypted, and translated through a series of three-dimensional matrices virtually augmented through the viewer using three orthogonal projections. Just don't ask what that means, I'm merely repeating what I was told. Programming and mathematics are a few more of my brother's passions. I really only know the basics of it, enough to know which way I need to proceed. It's probably hard to see from that angle, here..." Gnuella hands the screen to Ronnie.

From a direct eye level the viewer's depictions become clear and easy to understand. Three-dimensional arrows are virtually augmented along the ground directing where to proceed; she turns back-and-forth and around several times with her eyes affixed to the screen and is amazed that the projections remain in the same three-dimensional space as if they were directly painted to the ground. She turns the screen to her left to view what must have been the central portion of the city and notices that in the distance a face is projected unto one of the buildings. The face is strikingly familiar.

"What's this face?"

Gnuella leans over Ronnie's shoulder looking into the viewer and responds;

"My brother added that, it was a place we used to sneak off to when we were young. Now we sometimes use it as a safehouse when times become difficult. Only his and my viewers can decode that particular image. It's actually where our grandfather used to live."

Ronnie pulls the screen closer to her eyes and focuses tensely staring into the image. It's certainly a familiar face, but a few moments pass before she finally makes the connection.

It's Gramps.

NO ANDROID (TAKING THE HILL)

■ 12:47PM MARCH 2ND 3145

"So, I'm on another planet? And is it still the nineteen-eighties, or did that change to?"

Briskly walking the outer area of the alpha warehouses, Gramps takes full advantage of his newfound mobility. Looking around he can see, in the little light offered by the facilities scant exterior lighting system, that the building they'd just exited stretches hundreds of feet into the sky, and is in the southeastern quadrant of a small grid of four duplicate buildings.

"If you are referring to the year, it is currently thirty-one, forty-five. Would you like to know the month, day and time?"

"Thirty-one—No. Hell, better off not knowing—"

After glancing around once more, Norman continues;

"Know what a dog is Yursfon?"

Looking down at the little robot humming along at a matching pace he awaits a predictable reply.

"Dog? Dog—after searching the entire database allocated to my internal memory, I am afraid I cannot locate any information in regards to a *dog*. If you would like—"

Gramps, becoming increasingly annoyed, interrupts the robot, "Forget it! Didn't think you'd know."

"You got lights or somethin'? Can't see a dammed thing out here."

"Please refrain from speaking at such audible levels *Gramps*. My sensors indicate multiple unidentified trespassing subjects."

Taken aback, not only by the sudden direct response, but by its strange delivery, Gramps briefly looks around in the dark sky trying to pinpoint the origin of the robot's voice. It is almost as if the sounds were originating from within his head; certainly not from the robot's hovering shell.

With each unexplainable moment, Gramps becomes more and more frustrated.

Through wearing exasperation he replies;

"Where? If you're so damned observant, where are they?"

"Two-thousand, four-hundred, eighty-four meters south-east."

The unit replies precisely; again the sound seems to remain localized within the elderly man's ears.

"And how the hell could they hear us from that far away?"

"It is entirely within the realm of possibility, but certainty is completely dependent upon the specifics of the subjects detected. The *unidentified* subjects."

"Of all the smart-ass replies—if they're that far away how're they trespassin'?"

"Two-thousand, four-hundred, eighty-four meters south-east at the precise location of the intruders stands Prictex Premium^{ebr} Energy and Travel Service Center three, thirty-four. Though I am designed specifically to manage the alpha storage units, I am also obligated to investigate and report any anomalies occurring within Prictex Premium^{ebr} Energy and Travel Service Center three, thirty-four in the event that the service center operatives are not available."

Gramps replies gruffly;

"Well. I'm not obligated. I don't give a damn what happens at these prick-hole centers. An' why'n the hell are there no *operatives* available?"

"The center is no longer under operation. It has not yet been made clear to me if this is a temporary suspension or termination. Thus, I am, by design, to assume and proceed as if the center will resume operation at a later time. And you, I suspect, having no sense of your own whereabouts, would do best to stay in the company of one who does possess such familiarity. I may even be able to assist you further in locating '*Dog*' utilizing the service center's public information rectories."

Gramps shakes his head of vexation and responds;

"Fine, it's not like this crap could get any worse."

Just below the hovering robot, a dim white light shines into the soil and Yursfon speaks again in the same internally audible tones;

"This should maintain a low enough visibility to prevent our being discovered, and should suffice as a beacon to guide you. Follow and we will approach the invaders slowly and with great caution. They appear mostly stationary in their position, migrating occasionally within a small, three meter radius. If we proceed now, they should be within sight in twenty-three minutes. Please continue maintaining low audibility and keep close to the ground."

"Sir, yessir!"

Though condescension permeates the remark, Norman can't help but relate the circumstances to his days spent at war.

One-thousand, ninety-five meters pass with ease and sparse conversation until the elderly man and his accompanying assistance drone reach the foot of a steep hill.

"A possible vantage point, we may be able to locate and visualize the intruders from high ground."

A somewhat more genteel treatment of the sentiment than Norman would have heard from an army commanding officer, but still a common strategic choice.

"Yeah, might as well. Let's get this over with. Isn't there a headquarters or somethin' you can contact in case of emergency?"

"It would seem technical assistance has severed my communication with any external Prictex[ebr] networks or operatives."

Were it not the response of a robot, Norman would have considered the statement to be emotional, bearing a hint of depression. It seemed as if the unit was feeling dejected.

"Wonder why they'd go an' do a thing like that?"

"Please keep low to the ground. It is imperative that we conceal our presence."

Yursfon snaps back to the sarcastic query, disables his lights and proceeds slowly and silently towards the pinnacle of the mound.

The damned things got mood swings. Who ever heard of an emotional flying toolbox?

"Ya don't say. And here I was gonna yell '*Howdy*' and wave my arms at 'em."

Gramps follows the android crawling at an ever slowing speed with much greater effort exerted to remain inaudible in his movement.

"Unfortunately, it is now apparent. Such a lack of subtlety would have served us just as well. I believe the intruders are now aware of our presence".

Norman peers down the sloping vista and sees what resembles, albeit marginally, a service and fuel station. This vantage point allows him to can make out a few moving figures which appear to be retreating quickly into the station.

Mere seconds pass before the crowd once gracing the desert planet floor, are all contained within the apparent safety of the station.

A few muffled clunking and ringing noises surge along the terrain and funnel up the interior of the slope before connecting with Norman's ears.

He pauses to internally remark upon his somehow boosted senses, as if in distaste of the improvement.

Been a long time since I could see this far, and for once the ringing in my ear's actually comin' from somewhere. What the hell'd that talkin' toolbox do?

"What the hell was all that noise goin' on about?"

"The station has entered lock down and is now functioning under an internal reserve state. It appears at least one of its occupants is familiar with Prictex[ebr] proprietary firmware and has bypassed the standard security algorithms. I can no longer access the system as they have heavily encrypted the protocol now in place."

"So what now, tin man? Knock on the door and try to flank 'em?"

"The majority of my composition is titanium alloy and carbon steel. This is coated in a ceramic enamel film. Were I to be constructed of tin, I would not survive the levels of alkalis found in the Edirthaimian atmosphere. We should proceed to the station. I will inspect the exterior and search for another method of operation or perhaps discover a way to compromise the structure."

Yursfon once again enables his lightning system for Gramps' benefit and continues down the hill.

Norman follows the touchy unit with little reluctance. Having so little knowledge of his circumstances and surroundings has left him missing the luxury of harboring a stubborn and sometimes combative nature. On any other day in Bowling he would never take orders from what he perceives to be a personality-impaired machine. Of course, Norman admits to himself, a day in which he encounters a talking machine in Bowling, may just as likely find him in such a perplexed and frustrated state.

But at least I'd have The Quartzsite Bar.

"I sure could use a drink about now." Norman mutters to himself.

"You require a beverage? I currently contain nine liters and five-hundred milliliters of water ready for dispensing."

"Got any scotch? Or whiskey?"

Gramps again mocks the robot, expecting a technically coherent, but likely stupid reply.

"A form of alcohol? I can produce a tolerable amount of alcohol suitable for drinking through the expedited distillation of ethanol. I contain considerable percentages of the required carbon, hydrogen and oxygen atoms. These are stored, of course, for various uses in both daily routines and emergency circumstances. But I am capable of sparing the amount required to produce a suitable drink without inflicting too great of a loss on my chemical reserves. *A chemical depressant may reduce your contentious behavior.*"

This last remark is issued at a very low volume, likely for the unit's benefit and, if heard, for the elderly man's derision. As such is either not heard or is ignored by Norman, whose attention was at once ensnared and halted at the very beginning of the exposition.

"You got booze in there and you're just now telling me? Well, out with it, damnit. Let's find out if it's any good."

After three seconds conducted in silence a previously invisible compartment opens at the right-most hemisphere of the android's body producing a small cylindrical ampoule.

Retrieving the vial, Norman examines it momentarily in his hand.

"How do I open this damned thing?"

"Place the top of the ampoule in your mouth and inhale gently to extract the liquid."

Gramps follows the directions and draws a few sips.

"Ice cold; tastes more like dry gin than whiskey. Hell, it'll do in a pinch. Yurrie...I think you just became my favorite talkin' toaster."

Norman resumes sipping from the ampoule.

Such unlikely rapports have never been so simply formed.

Thus the remaining distance is travelled with no further complaints from the elderly man.

■ 1:21AM MARCH 3RD 3145

The old man and the storage maintenance unit stand just before the entrance of the station, now completely fortified and to Gramps' eyes, impregnable.

"So, figured out how to get in there?"

"At this vicinity I am able to interface directly with the emergency access. However, it seems rather reluctant to comply with my requests."

"Didn't we already go through this? I thought we were going to find some way to break in."

"It was my intention to first attempt interaction with the emergency access, as even when damaged or compromised it usually greets my requests with friendly obedience once I have been assigned the proper security administrative clearance. I had hoped the intruders would have overlooked this access, with its lack of visibility and its existence being concealed in all but the lowest security administrative levels of the systems internal framework. I am proceeding with an exhaustive structural composition scan."

"You do that, Yurrie."

Gramps finally finishes his third ampoule and tosses the empty to the unit. Yursfon refills the vial with water and has gradually been watering down the alcoholic drink to prevent an incoherent state of intoxication in the man, whom Yursfon believes may yet prove useful.

"An' don't think I haven't noticed. You've been watering down my drinks."

"Yes, I have, we need to—"

"I ain't stupid, I've been to war. We need to keep our wits. You any good in combat? Or do you think that's what this'll come to? An old man and a talkin' beverage machine..."

Norman chuckles and shakes his head in dismayed amusement.

"I once terminated twenty-three intruders."

"Wait, what'n the hell? You tellin' me you've killed people? A two-foot tall flying breadbox?"

"Not people, *intruders*. I terminated twenty-three life-forms measuring an average of sixty-six centimeters each, after finding they were occupying both the storage units and the service station without proper admittance. They would not listen to reason and with their four large incisors masticated portions of Prictex Premium[ebr] stock, some wiring, and various containment vessels. When confronting such species, I am programmed to eradicate and prevent repopulation."

If the android possessed the ability to express pride, he would be beaming with it.

"So you exterminated some vermin, like any other groundskeeper. What the hell use is that now?"

"I am merely confirming my ability to terminate intruders, if designated necessary."

"Yeah, well, killing somebody's a whole lot different from trapping some damn rats."

"There may be a significant sociological distinction, but the contrasts in difficulty of termination between species are considerably slight."

"You're gonna start scarin' me Yurrie. Let's just get movin'."

"I've finished scanning the structural composition of the station, it appears that this section of the station may be compromised. Erosion developed through the apparent porous construction of this particular section, probably due to an error during the manufacturing process has considerably diminished the wall's integrity."

"Dammit Yurrie. Start talkin' sense already."

"I can destroy this wall and thus impregnate the station. Please retreat to a distance of at least fifteen meters."

Norman sighs with great exaggeration, but complies nonetheless.

"Hey, wait a minute, what about you?"

Norman shouts as if he'd surpassed audible range.

"No need to shout. I can hear you quite clearly. Once I have implanted the explosive compound within the wall, I will be allocated sixty seconds for my retreat. I will only require forty-six point three."

With that Y-R-S – F-N forty-two begins drilling into the side of the station's worn exterior with an intensely focused optical laser. The hole stretches twenty-three centimeters into the wall and is quickly filled with a large concentration of hydrogen gas, sealed with a rapidly expanding carbon gel. With the internal temperature of the wall not being great enough to cause ignition of the gas; Yursfon affixes a heating disc to the wall, timed to reach five-hundred degrees Celsius in exactly sixty seconds.

A powerful, but quiet shot is heard in the momentary silence. A great fissure tears through the air in a straight line behind a super-heated projectile which pierces the rear exterior of Yursfon's shell, defeating the ceramics, titanium and carbon with little effort. As suddenly as the robot turns to retreat, he collapses to the old star-beaten floor just before the wall.

"Yurrie!"

Norman shouts even louder than before, but stands paralyzed staring at the disabled android. He means to run and rescue the robot in some daring, reckless act, but another part of him restricts this gesture of suicidal heroics.

I haven't found Pete yet. I haven't found Tim. And after all, even though I kinda like 'im, it's just a robot.

The wall explodes. Norman braces himself and shields his face with his arms, still reeling from the shot. He opens his eyes and stares towards the entrance of the station as the dust slowly clears.

"What the hell'd you go an' do that for? Yurrie's just a goddamn talkin' drink-mixer."

Shouting again with his voice cracking slightly from a mild lapse of emotional response, he fails to keep at bay. Norman watches through what remains of the thicket of dust.

The station's external lighting systems activate and a tall, slender shape stands just before the station entrance with arms raised and both hands clasped tightly around a pistol pointed at the old man. After a few seconds pass, the dust is completely settled and the figure dons all visible details in the bright artificial light. A young dark-skinned woman of about twenty stares at Norman with piercing green eyes, as her crimson and amber hair dances across her face in excited rhythm with the tepid gusts of desert air.

"Give me a break! I'm gonna die bein' shot by a girl."

"Yah adham duune tokk swey!"

The young woman demands with a firm, but lilting voice, then steps forward slowly with her arms still erect and narrows her eyes at Norman in intense focus.

"And she can't even tell me in English, what the hell I'm dyin' for."

The station door opens and a young dark-haired boy sharing the young woman's eye color and complexion, takes his stand just beside her and translates;

"She said; '*You have come to kill us.*'"

Norman sighs again as he is increasingly becoming accustomed to the feeling of exasperation.

"Listen here, kid. I ain't come here to kill nobody. I don't even know where'n the hell *here* is. I just wanna find my damned dog and be on my way."'

"The Y-R-S, F-N model has made multiple attempts to contact this districts Prictex security network. If it's discovered that we are trespassing here, we'll be enslaved or killed. The android wouldn't understand our situation and our need for shelter. I wouldn't be able to keep interfering with its signal without its becoming aware."

Norman gestures to the woman.

"So you have this one kill him? Yurrie wouldn't have given you up if you would've just talked to him. Hell, I'm trespassin' and he's been fixin' me drinks."

"Yurrie?"

The boy questions Norman, briefly glancing up at the young woman to see that her guard, like his, is easing.

"The robot thing. Look, I wake up in the middle of nowhere, he's the only thing around that can talk…and it takes too damn long to spell out all that garbage."

"So you're not with the Prictex people?"

"I just started hearing that damn Prictex crap. I ain't with nobody."

The boy turns around and reenters the station leaving the door open for the woman who holsters her pistol, and beckons quickly at Norman to follow, lightly commands the same;

"Auftarr!"

Norman walks towards the entrance and stops, turning to the emaciated debris that once was unit Y-R-S – F-N forty-two and bends to retrieve a small shard of the robots shell. Still hot from the blast, he wraps it in a handkerchief and places it in his pocket. The young woman patiently waits beside the entrance watching with curiosity.

"Auftarr." She repeats, softly this second time.

Norman complies and follows the young woman into the station.

■ 2:03AM MARCH 3RD 3145

Stepping into the dark room, just behind his tall guide, Norman glances hurriedly back and forth with an unease born in the darkness. He does not know exactly why he's been so compliant in what seems like an unending series of increasingly unusual and frankly frustrating events. It is not in his nature, and he finds himself just as bewildered with his own behavior as with the strange proceedings. His mind has been preoccupied with thoughts of his lost loved ones and the resulting need to reach out to seize those who have slipped his grasp. The possibility that he may yet commit his one last act of valor provides a drive long omitted and long believed to be permanently re-moved from his life. With this, he figures, some bewilderment and uncertainty can be tolerated.

The lighting system inside of the service station is activated and every corner, crevice, and nook in the room is illuminated with a bright, artificial tinge. The room is mostly barren and re-minds Norman of a waiting room in an intensive care unit, even that same sense of depression and unease seems to be present.

Five figures all sharing the same darkly toned skin, stand before him; the two he'd previously witnessed, the tall young woman and the small English-speaking boy, along with a large woman with altogether darker features which appear to be lightening due to age and an apparent illness, a young girl with strikingly bright blonde-white hair, and another child who's gender is not immediately identifiable. Norman thinks it to be another girl, but her auburn hair is short and disheveled accom-panying a scraggy, boyish demeanor.

It's a family. A sickly old woman and her four children. Where the hell's the father?

The small boy steps forward without hesitation and pro-ceeds to introduce the group quickly and methodically, as if to hurry through the social formality.

"My name is Arcos Giiandheres and this is my family."

Arcos begins pointing to each figure as he names them to the old stranger. Starting with the tall woman who'd just mo-ments before had the intruder in her pistol sights;

"My sister Vinda, mother Pauless, and my other two sisters Anika and Brasiil."

All, with odd, but somehow fitting names, even the last whose gender is now made clear, begin to stare at the stranger expectantly.

"Guess it's my turn. Name's Norman Donaldson. Most peo-ple call me Gramps..."

Norman mutters a few inaudible words and continues;

"Ah hell, I guess you might as well call me Gramps too."

Vinda, though not entirely sure of what was said, smiles at the comical and alien way in which the old man delivered his words.

Arcos looks up at his older sister and decides to let down his guard as well with a quick laugh.

"Gramps it is."

"Yeah, yeah..."

Looking down with a momentary pause, Gramps allows himself a brief consideration for the belated Yursfon.

In a hurried and sincere tone, Vinda quavers softly;

"Washe Doun Betarnii teka."

"She says she's sorry for destroying the android. Your... friend?"

"Bah, that talking toaster—He helped me out that's all. I don't know where the hell I am or what's goin' on. He offered to help me find my friends. You killed 'em, so, I figure, you're gonna be helpin' in his stead."

"How have you come to be here, that you don't know where here is?"

"What the hell is that, a riddle? I don't know. I was in the backyard of my house in Arizona, in the good ol' 'U', 'S' of 'A'. It was that black mess that brought me here. That's my best guess, anyway."

"Black mess? You mean the Dirac matter?"

Moving closer while looking up at Gramps, Arcos poses the question with a striking curiosity.

"You know, most of the words even *you* say sound like goofenthal to me. An' stand back some, I'm gonna start thinkin' ya ain't right in the head if ya keep gettin' so close to me."

Gramps takes a small step back away from the boy.

"It was some black tar or somethin' on the floor of my garage, looked like I didn't know how to take care of my vehicles..."

Gramps pauses as if awaiting laughter after a punchline.

"Anyway, I've seen the stuff eat a shotgun, it almost ate me. I know damn well it ate Tim, an' my dog Pete. I climbed into it thinkin'—I don't know, I'd find 'em somehow. It sounds kinda stupid ta say it out loud."

Gramps finishes this short bout with; "So that's my story."

"Follow me."

The boy abruptly leads the way to the door with his older sister in tow. The rest of the family seems perfectly content to stay behind.

"Alrighty. Got no reason not to, right?"

Outside of the station Arcos, leads the two to the edge of a cliff a few minutes southeast of the building. He points down beyond and stares intently.

"There! Dirac matter."

Gramps reluctantly approaches the edge of the cliff noticing Vinda makes no such attempts. Standing beside the boy he looks down and sees the quivering mass of black matter.

"Holy hell! Well, that's the crap that I jumped into. It weren't no sea, just a puddle."

"You jumped into it...and were transported here?"

The boy steps closer and leans forward seemingly entranced by the black ocean. As the fine soil beneath his feet gives way, he slips. Before he plummets to what would likely be his doom, Gramps throws his arms around the boy's chest and pulls him up in a clumsy rescue.

Vinda races to join the two and sighs in relief at her brother's safety. Standing over the two, she lightly offers;

"Dekonii."

Gramps releases Arcos who translates his sister's shared sentiment;

"Thanks."

He then peers up at the old man and again implants a small amount of unease within Gramps.

Dumb kid's too fascinated by this crap, doesn't know he should be afraid of it.

"Yeah. Yeah."

A pause allows Gramps, now sitting on the edge of the cliff with the boy and his sister, to become transfixed by the sight of an ocean of the most perplexing material ever to grace the universe.

"Now, stop starin' at me."

ISOLATION (LAST KNOWN SURROUNDINGS)

■ (TIME/DATE)

Jill wakes to a riotous sound of thunder in the distance. Her head is currently attempting to break its own record with one of the worst migraines she's ever experienced. She sits up, closes her eyes and palms her head;

"Ow—Ah! That was so stupid. What were we thinking Eddie—?"

Jill opens her eyes, bats her head and shifts her sight quickly to find that she is surrounded by absolute darkness.

"EDDIE!"

No reply.

"MIKE!"

Again, no reply. At any other moment, in any other situation, she might be grateful for a lack of Michael, but Jill finds herself quickly wishing for any familiar person to accompany her in the dark unease.

Standing, Jill puts both arms out before her, and attempts to feel around for something solid to brace and guide her along.

No such luck.

Nothing meets her hand as she turns herself around feeling for anything in her immediate vicinity. She decides to walk in the direction she currently faces, having no possible sense of what direction that may be.

With her hands still flailing about her she catches one along the sharp edge of a metal shard and quickly jerks both arms back. Using one hand to investigate the other she finds that the scratch is minor and did not draw blood. Even so, she keeps her hands to her chest, not wishing to injure herself if at all avoidable.

Instead, she walks slowly, keeping her steps very close to one another and only committing to each step once the ground below is felt to be secure.

Four minutes pass at this sluggish pace and she decides to once again break the silence.

"Eddie, Mike, anybody! I can't see a thing!"

Jill focuses her mind upon pleasant memories of Eddie and her parents not wishing to allow it to stray into panic-inducing mental realms.

The silence doesn't help.

"Someone say something. Even Michael, no matter how stupid it may be."

A low cackle and groan echoes from some distant corner of the room.

Jill stops and shivers at the sound.

The cackle returns and lifts in volume into a continuous screech, spanning eighteen, otherwise silent, seconds.

Sounds of glass breaking under foot and rubble aggressively forced aside batter Jill's already frayed nerves.

She can think of only one course of action; probably reckless, likely unwise, but very common as a response to such circumstances.

Jill runs.

Continuing in the same direction, she once lightly toddled without so much concern. She bolts as if the sound is immediately behind her breathing hateful intentions just short of her back and making attempts to grab and pull her into its dominion of reveling anguish, with her only solace found in the simple assurance that whatever happens to her, she will not see a thing.

She bursts without stumble for what seems like miles, though merely meters, before she perceives something in the darkness before her. A blue light suspended at a height greater than her own, forming the letters 'A' and 'F', followed by the number fifteen. Above this, an animated depiction in a similar blue color, of what looks to be a supply pallet being carted unto a lift, can be seen as a saving grace. An elevator, no matter its purpose, is a great way to escape pursuit.

Jill stops abruptly just before throwing herself full-speed into the lift door. She looks around hurriedly and finds a green lighted sphere far below and to the left of the lighted displays.

A button.

She hopes and presses her finger into the translucent, ethereal green ball.

The lift opens, lighting the way.

"Thank God!"

Jill considers for moment turning around to look behind her with the light revealing her pursuer but dares not, steps in and waits for the door to close behind her.

■ (SOMETIME LATER)

"What the hell? Don't those totally look like—?"

"Yeah I know." Eddie interjects before Mike finishes a series of questions that either party couldn't possibly answer.

Nevertheless, Michael continues his pointless verbalization of predictable inquiries as he follows Eddie out of the container with thoughtless automation.

"I mean what's that all about in there? Why Ronnie? You think she's here, or somethin'? Where' we goin' anyway?"

"Damnit Mikey! How the hell should I know? I just got here, the same way you did. Same damned time. Where's Jill? You seen her? Last thing we need is to lose somebody else."

"Nah, Eddie. Sorry, I think we lost her after we did whatever the hell we just did."

Mike pats Eddies shoulder and swivels his head looking around the devastation that was once a dominating structure.

His gaze returns to the container, the only object of any discernible interest to be seen.

"Shit! Of course, what the hell am I doing?"

Muttering as he proceeds, Eddie wanders aimlessly deeper into the building.

"Eddie, you hear that?"

Eddie turns back to see Mike standing beside the container looking towards a small hatch they'd not noticed before. Buried behind debris, the slick metallic surface of a top corner frame and a portion of a door could be seen.

"I don't really hear anything."

Shortly after Eddie says this, his ears correct him, finding the sound and tuning in to decipher what he equates to metal grinding upon metal and clambering into a screech as the source apparently nears.

Both men approach the hatch and take cover behind a large blue slab of iridized steel.

The screeching sound of metallic friction becomes more audible and defined. It is the accompanied by the unmistakable sound of a woman screaming for her life.

After exchanging glances, the two again affix their stares to the small metal door, both sharing the assumption that the sound is that of a lift carriage with a single occupant plummeting to their ground level.

Eddie runs to the hatch and begins throwing the smaller debris aside. Mike assists and together the men clear most of the debris from the door which is clearly intended for the transportation of inventory, not people.

■ (EVEN LATER THAN BEFORE)

Inside the cramped lift, Jill clings to the brace along the wall behind her and rips through her vocal chords with a strenuous shriek. The lift begins tilting as it falls in an attempt to compensate for the one-sided weight within. The minor rotation causes the top corner and opposing bottom corner to grate along the interior walls of the shaft generating friction heat which tries to escape in the form of sparks.

As the grinding elevator carriage scours away just enough of its edges to allow another slight rotation, it becomes lodged and slows to a stop just before meeting the ground level.

Jill continues screaming a few additional seconds before realizing her plummet has ended with her still intact.

"Oh dear God!"

She feels around in the darkness until her hands meet the wall supporting her. Slowly she climbs up, back to the wall, with her hands as her guide and balance support.

Breathing quickly and deeply, she recovers from the shock and with what little remains of her voice, yells once more in desperation;

"Help! Is anybody out there? I'm stuck inside."

Michael, reminded of a favored song, recites a few lyrics before emitting a high-pitched and decidedly discomforting wail, trying to mimic the song's backing vocals.

"Shut up Mike! JILL? Is that you?"

As he touches along the frame of the door Eddie attempts to find or feel some way to open the hatch.

"Eddie! Thank God! I'm stuck inside the elevator. It shut down right when I climbed in. And just—"

"It's alright, just stay calm. Mikey, help me with this door."

"How?"

"I don't know. Instead of just standing there singing Pink Floyd you could help me find a way."

Michael proceeds to kick the door, which responds making an audible clunk echoing through the shaft.

"What was that?"

To Jill the sound is amplified greatly, and when she considers that the lift has not yet reached the ground, she finds the sound to be intimidating.

"It was Mike being a dipshit. Can you tell where you are? It sounded like you hit the ground."

"Mike, do that again and I'LL KILL YOU!"

Jill attempts to stand upright, but loses her balance and returns to the safety of the wall lean.

"It's too dark in here, I can't see anything and I don't really want to move."

"That's okay just stay put. We'll figure something out. The door is just one straight piece of metal. There's no handle or buttons or anything."

Eddie places his open palms on the smooth metallic surface of the door and tries to pull the hatch open with what little adherence his clammy hands achieve through suction and pressure.

Mike repeats the attempt from the opposite direction after Eddie fails.

"No go. OPEN UP, YOU PEI—"

The door opens responding to the vocalized 'open' command.

"No shit. Just had to use the magic word. You're welcome Jill."

Leaning in through the hatch, Mike looks up the shaft to see the bottom of the lift just above his head.

"Fuck. The elevator's stuck."

Michael pulls out of the hatch entry just as Eddie leans in to verify the statement.

"Hold on just a little longer Jill. We've got the door open, but the elevator's stuck just above the hatch."

"No hurry. I'm having a blast in here and it only kind of smells like pee and 'B. O.'"

Being a lift intended for the transport of various goods once received, generated, and distributed at the Omni Networks, Tascert Subdivision known as Aethra Center, the odor is not the aged residue of human urine or other human bodily dispersions.

Rather, the odor is due in large measure to a single incidence occurring over six-hundred years prior.

An artificial lifeform developed around this time had become popular as a household pet.

The Tardisect, as it was known, required no maintenance and subsided on bacteria extracted from airborne particles and also those subsequently generated through modified and patented unilocular cells, of which it was primarily composed. In addition to its general use, the Tardisect's composition meant it could be used to remove unwanted bacteria from living spaces, thus making it all-the-more desirable.

Another feature patented by the Omni Network Tascert Subdivision; Tardisects, when compressed, would generate heat through a trademarked use of multilocular adipocyte cells. A feature children enjoyed greatly. Unlike most manufactured and stuffed animals fit for use as sleeping partners, the Tardisect better resembled a living pet with the advantage of requiring no upkeep.

While it looked much like a lumpy, white, six-legged naked mole rat with tentacles resembling the appendages of an anemone, it emitted varying bioluminescent colors and would hum pleasant ambient sounds chirping from time to time, helping it to secure its popularity with children as a sleeping aid.

It was by all measures a commercial hit, one of many for the Aethra Center.

However, because it needed to excrete a compound comprised of ammonia, proteins, bacteria and chloride to survive, it was infused with a superheated eradication system contained within a platinized ceramic-based insulator attached to the hindquarters of the creature. Though the insulator was largely considered indestructible, it would in fact, break from time to time when under extreme duress.

When a Tardisect broke free of its shipping case, while being transported in the lift Jill finds herself occupying, it climbed into the lifted base of a large-battery transport pallet, only to be crushed by the weight of the batteries when the lifted base closed in response to the inventory lift coming to an abrupt stop due to a later resolved malfunction.

Unfortunately, this resulted with the Tardisect evacuating its insides into its insulation chamber, which simultaneously cracked and erupted before having the opportunity to eradicate the material as intended.

Though the elevator was cleaned vigorously afterwards, the residual stench of these excreted materials would forever remain within its walls.

Mike retrieves his lighter and hands it to Eddie.

"Hold this under the elevator."

Eddie complies and leans over the door frame, positioning himself just far enough into the shaft to hold the lighter within one inch from the bottom of the lift.

Michael climbs into the shaft using metal paneling and exposed pipes as footholds.

Using a small standard pocket screwdriver Michael pries open a circuitry panel on the undercarriage of the lift and begins.

Without hesitation or pause to consider possible solutions ,Michael proceeds manipulating and rerouting the circuitry in a matter of only few masterfully spent minutes. To Eddie, it is as if Michael is channeling some brilliant technician whose very nature is predisposed to all things electronic.

Exactly four minutes pass before the lift responds and lights up the interior of shaft. Michael quickly climbs back through the hatch just before the lift resumes its attempted descent.

"You never fail to amaze me, Mikey. That was really something."

Eddie casually tosses the lighter back to its owner.

"Just hope it's got enough power to force its way down. It looked pretty jammed up."

Michael turns to Eddie and continues with a stern expression and very solemn tone; "Where the hell are we, Eddie?"

"Like I said, I don't know any more than you...What's with you anyway?"

"That lift isn't connected to anything. It's powering itself, but there's no power source anywhere, nothing. I couldn't figure it out."

Scratching his head, Michael stares at the barely moving lift.

"Hey, you got it working."

Eddie slaps Michael's back and nods to him.

"That was easy. I just bypassed a fried wire. That's some serious shit in there."

"I don't get you. Those projections of Veronica, or whatever they are, don't seem to strike you as bat-shit crazy, but some elevator circuits—"

"No shit. It's weird. I guess I wasn't even thinkin' about it, not 'til I saw that."

Mike points to the lift just as it becomes dislodged and abruptly drops below the entryway with the door opening providing just enough space to allow Jill to slip through with Eddie's help.

Jill stands and dusts herself.

"What is all this? Eddie, none of this makes sense."

She turns to Michael who appears to be bewildered;

"Thanks Mike."

Michael fails to respond. Instead he turns his back to the couple and proceeds to the unit containing various likenesses of his best friend's girl.

"What's with him?"

Turning to Eddie, Jill lightly pecks his cheek.

"Mike's finally joined the real world. For the first time in his life, I think."

"That's scary. Is he out of smoke?"

Eddie chuckles briefly to Jill's response and holds her hand, gently squeezing it.

■ DATE/TIME NOT YET CERTAIN

"Hey Jill! You should come check this out!"

Michael bellows from within the container.

The Chapels approach the container and look inside to find Michael standing over and touching the face of one of the projections he's removed from its containing case.

"What? What is this? Mike don't touch that."

Jill stands back at the opening to the shipping unit as Eddie climbs in with Michael.

"Eddie, they're not just projections, it feels like actual skin. This shit's crazy."

Reaching out, Mike attempts to press his index finger into the left eye of the artificial being, but is halted as Eddie grabs his arm.

"Don't do that. That's creepy."

Instead, Eddie flicks a finger across the short virtual red hair.

"What in—"

"Can I do something for you, baoshwee?" A cadent and sultry voice, bearing an accent resembling, to Eddie, a combination of French and South African, issues the question.

The virtual woman opens her eyes and quickly darts her soft red irises and deep black pupils to the top left of her eyelids focusing intensely upon Eddie's face.

"Holy shit!"

Michael blurts out as the two men quickly jump and stumble backwards, with Eddie kicking the platform into the wall in his fumble.

"Fuck me man! That chick just talked."

"I'm aware."

Eddie stands upright and tries to regain composure.

Jill snickers quietly and joins, completing the group in a semi-circle around the tipped projection.

"Would you mind standing me back up Queelling, or do you like me better on my back?"

The virtual woman, dressed in unusual, but provocative attire, winks at Michael, to whom she directs the question. Michael eyes the teal and red figure which appears to be wearing two thin streams of tightly adhering, almost painted-on fabrics, that stretch from a straight horizontal cut just above each breast and intersect somewhere between the legs.

"Are you seriously checking out a hologram, or whatever that is?"

In disapproval, Jill shakes her head adding;

"I can't get over how much it looks like Veronica."

Eddie grasps the small disc-like projection base, propped crookedly on the wall and returns it to a standing position. The figure, having appeared to also be leaning on the nearby wall, bending then returning to a stance with fluid, life-like and even provocative movements performed in tandem with the repositioning of the projection base.

"What's your name?"

Michael asks as the other two stare, both wondering if an artificial construct intended to look, sound and feel human would have a name, or if, like other products purchased and delivered in shipping cases, the name is nonexistent unless designated by the purchaser.

"My name is Vianise Ambrosine Ripuaron. I'm a model H-A-I-L, V-R, two-eight-one operating on HALTSEC firmware version two point eight-one point one point one-zero-zero-three-two. Most prefer to call me 'V. R.'"

After relating her lengthy and likely inconsequential identification information, Vianise crosses her legs and curtsies.

"What's your pleasure?"

"Whoa! This thing's totally flirting with me. It's like some kind of sex worker or somethin'."

"Shut up Mike, you moron."

Nudging Eddie and Michael aside, Jill steps in closely to the animated three-dimensional representation of the female form.

"What kind of services do you provide?"

Eddie looks quizzically at his wife, with whom he is so intimately familiar he is able to surmise a sudden arousal of very specific and calculated intentions. However, it is not clear in any way, what these intentions may be.

"What are you doing, Jill?"

"Anything you may desire. I am quite capable of either personal and intimate relationships or purely carnal liaisons."

The projected Miss Ripuaron leans in very closely to Jill and caresses her face with her left hand. Jill steps back, thoroughly disturbed by the implication and the strangely soft, delicate and nearly human touch.

"Or...If that's not your thing." Vianise smirks.

"I am connected to a live network of over three-hundred billion information feeds updated regularly. So, if you have questions, of any kind, I would be more-than-willing to tell you anything you need to know. I was designed with the ability to analyze and discuss any number of topics from mathematics to socio-economic affairs. Is there anything, baoshwee, you would like to discuss?"

The voice begins with a distinct sense of pragmatism and sincerity, but as the AI continues, she institutes notes of ambiguity leading into further attempts at emotional provocation.

"No? I also garner a thorough and regularly updated understanding of the neurological and psychological human constructs. You may confide in me, and I'd love to advise you."

Jill interrupts what would have been an exhaustive, but likely stimulating explanation of every possible service the incredibly intelligent humanoid system has to offer.

"Alright, I get it. You're a prostitute, *I don't even want to think of how that would work*. A library, a newspaper, and a psychiatrist all bundled into this overtly promiscuous package."

Jill, practically skewering the words, stares with narrowed eyes into the unaffected, and, in fact, still smirking face of the brightly glowing projection.

"Jeez Jill. Take it easy."

Only once before had Eddie heard the condemning and demeaning tone from his wife; when she was first introduced to Veronica.

"Catfight!"

"Shut up Mike!"

Jill snaps back at the also smirking man.

"I bet you're a locator and a directory too. Right?"

"Of course, in fact—"

Vianise attempts to continue in response to Jill's question, only to be interrupted by her once more.

"Right. So answer these questions for us. Where are we? What year is it? Do the name Veronica Rawls or Timmothy Chapel mean anything to you? Oh, and what the hell are these words, *'bahow-shween'* and *'kweel-ling'* or however you said them."

"I'd love to tawllily."

Jill is certain this additional word is introduced by the cyber nymph with the singular intent of annoying her.

"We are in the Aethra Center, located at twelve-eighty-five dash sub-A, and Y-O-C dot forty-seven, Masadoix City, Antweran. Less precisely, the Endourixan continent in the western hemisphere of Earth."

Jill looks to Eddie and Mike, both sharing the same perplexed appearance as Vianise continues;

"The year is thirty-one, twenty-three A. D. Nine-thirty six PM, October twenty-forth."

■ 9:36PM OCTOBER 24TH 3123

"I'm glad you guys are here too, or I'd be thinkin' I need to cut back on my shit."

Mike attempts to force a smile and a moment of comedic relief into the now daunting atmosphere.

He is met with no accompanying laughter or ease from his friends. Only a continuation of discomforting silence.

"A baoshwee is an attractive and desirable individual, as is a tawllily, the colloquialisms more feminine form. Now, a queelling is one who is sweet, cute and oh, so simple."

Vianise approaches Michael with an amatory sway and once her body is fixed mere centimeters from his, she strokes his chin with her finger.

"Michael. She just called you stupid."

Jill interrupts the virtual enticement and Vianise, again, returns to her base.

"I'm afraid I can offer no information in the regards of Veronica Rawls or Timmothy Chapel. Do you forgive me? I'd love to help you with anything else. Anything at all."

Again, the holographic life-form attempts to use alluring behavior to redirect the group's attention.

Jill, of course, is provoked rather than seduced and responds with further questioning.

"I thought you had access to any information we wanted. You've no information on these two people, none at all. There's probably like eighty million people with either of these names, not to mention the fact that you're Veronica's doppelganger. Can you explain that?"

Eddie not only approves of the line of questioning, but finds himself almost ashamed that he'd not once thought to proceed with similar questions, knowing that he was likely manipulated, if only momentarily, by the being's erogenous conduct, and deftly so.

"Oh, I can give all of the information needed regarding the numerous Timmothy Chapels and Veronica Rawls that have ever existed throughout time, but I suspect there are two specific individuals for whom you are searching. These two are likely the same two about whom information is very off-limits. Tantalizing, isn't it?"

Further amorous conduct follows the oddly admissive response.

"But, I'm afraid I can't help you, unless…"

V-R leans in very closely, meeting Jill eye-to-eye.

"You can give your name."

"Jill Chapel." Answers unflinching.

Vianise returns to an erect stance over the platform and giggles;

"I thought as much. And these two gentlemen must be Edward Chapel and Michael Brenham."

AWAKE (AND SANITY IS WANING)

Tim's head is, once again, throbbing. He figures he may as well get used to the ever more common headache, as it seems increasingly unlikely he'll make it through any great stretch of time without encountering another strange creature or substance with intentions to harm him.

He sits with his eyes shut, reluctant to move in any way. It is made immediately clear to him, with little effort spent in the discovery; his wrists and ankles are bound, tightly. It seems movement was never much of an option.

Opening his eyes, as it is one of the few acts he may still commit, Tim rolls them along their spherical curves to the top of his lids in an attempt to perceive, with waning focus, and possibly waning sanity. The alien face, of a very strange looking man standing just over him, far too close for comfort.

"You gonna hit me in the head again? You stupid pricks won't let up, will you?"

Silence.

Tim finds great difficulty in focusing his eyes, but can plainly see that the figure before him has made no movement in response to his comment.

"If you're just gonna stand there, would you kindly do me a favor and FUCK OFF!"

Tim tries to lunge forward, but catches in his bondage, reminding him that he is being held firmly to the wall behind.

He closes his eyes in exasperation, but cannot seem to quiet himself so simply;

"Dammit. What the hell do you want from me? You're creepin' me out just standing there."

Silence once more, as the figure seems content to simply stand and stare.

"Give me a break."

Tim leans back and rolls his head along the wall. He begins laughing with an acute coupling of frustration and despondency.

"Day-ous-sin bea-line saul-do-soss rok-ma-rot?"

"Ah, what the hell...If that shit's how you talk, then forget I said anything and just keep your damned mouth shut."

With his blurred eyesight Tim cannot be certain, but at a later time of reflection, he'd swear he watched the man remove a tooth, twist and squeeze it, then return the tooth into the vacant socket of his gums.

"I apologize for that. An old version of those PrictMed Oral Linquistulators. *Doesn't even work half of the time!* Piece of junk it is. Leave it to Prictex to release *such garbage* before beta testing it."

With this response the stranger increases emphasis almost disproportionately with various phrases, and at other times trails off with quickly fading inflection. It's an unusual, but somehow familiar tendency, in that it reminds Tim of the accents he'd sometimes heard from those of Eastern European backgrounds, back when he was still on Earth. How long ago that, now, seems to be.

The not-quite-human leans down and begins looking Tim over very closely, shifting around from side to side examining his face, body and bindings.

"Anyway, I merely meant to ask *if you were human*. I'm now certain you are, so no need to worry about that, *eh*?"

Tim flinches and pulls back as the man reaches for his face, but is incredibly limited in his movement and too weary to resist much more.

"*By the great Krah-pock-fles!* Those bastards really worked you over, didn't they? Good thing for you *I came along!* But then again, I was supposed to find you."

With both hands wrapped tightly around Tim's head, the stranger presses both thumbs gently under each eye and holds them with a light pressure for a few seconds. Tim watches with amazement as his eyes regain focus.

"Now, you can *at least see me*, as scary a sight as that may be."

The stranger lets out a singular raucous laugh that leaves Tim feeling greater unease than had already been afforded.

"*I am Xakdrekai Nuregstein!* You?"

Tim peers up to clearly see the man now attempting to remove his bindings and is startled by the sight. Crouching before him, he sees a humanoid creature with an illuminated, pulsing and bulbous protuberance on either side of his head. They seem to heave in tandem with thin filaments of folded, fissured tissue opening and closing rapidly. These punctuate the temples; peripheral of an otherwise human face, with dark brown, curly hair extending beyond the head in the shape of a round cloud, a similar colored goatee and hazel eyes. The skin however, when lighted by the bioluminescent orbs, appears to be a light ashen blue.

As Xakdrekai turns back and forth manipulating the bonds securing Tim to the cell wall, Tim notices the being's ears are unusually large and taper to a point at the top of the pinna.

Alien.

But not completely.

"Uh...Tim."

He stares deeply into the unusual growth, glowing so brightly it illuminates his own face as well as Xakdrekai's.

"Son of a bitch."

Tim jerks his hands up and rubs his raw and bloody wrists, not yet considering the implication that they are free to do so.

"Sorry Tim. The bindings were really tight. *Enough to break the skin, even!*"

In the distance, several large footsteps can be heard along with obnoxious and boisterous conversations spoken in some unfamiliar language.

"*Oy nah-bee-shaw!* They're coming back. Put your hands behind your back and pretend they're still bound."

Tim complies with the stranger's whispered request and hangs his head trying his best to portray a sullen and languid prisoner. An act, but only a slight exaggeration of his current disposition.

"Ah. Well done, *my friend!* I must hide momentarily. But I will return, and finish *with the rescuing!*"

Watching as his strange new savior slinks into the darkness, Tim observes the glow of Xakdrekai's skull waiver and disappear, leaving only black. Tim surmises that somewhere in his surroundings, some form of holding cell, is hidden a passage through ductwork or possibly drainage pipes as the room does bear a musty, stagnate odor which tends to accompany standing water.

Though Tim can now see clearly, he finds the room is far too dark without the light of Xakdrekai's head. He can distinguish no further details of his surroundings and has only the option to wait, in silent darkness, for the arrival of his would-be captors through some unseen cell entrance.

I was better off unconscious.

Tim considers this thought and recalls the numerous times he'd forcefully hastened his loss of consciousness through various chemical means.

For a moment he wanders into another train of thought starting with the realization that he may never again have the chance to be so inebriated.

He may never see Ronnie again...or his brother, Gramps, Mikey, the bar, or even Jill; *but I could probably go a few years without being called a dickhead all the time.*

Fuck it, I miss em' all.

Tim lays his head back upon the cell wall and can feel as a few stray tears trudge slowly through the grime and dust now masking his youthful face.

"What the hell did I even do? I must've pissed off too many people."

With his head aimed as thoroughly to the ceiling as his position, and sight will allow, Tim continues;

"I guess that's it. I'm just paying for something stupid I've done. Right?"

Tim slinks his head back down and lets it hang loosely.

"Why isn't Mikey here? He does stupid shit all the time."

Tim pauses releasing a sigh.

"God damns the lucky ones."

Tim, at various times in his youth, was given, by Richard, this piece of supposed wisdom. It never made much sense but Eddie tried to explain their father's enigmatic sentiment in simple terms; *'He means you can only have it so easy for so long, eventually the shit has to hit the fan. You can't skate by on dumb luck forever'.*

'Tim, you gotta grow up. Get a job. Stop counting on everybody else. You're lucky you got a brother like Eddie. But God damns the lucky ones'.

"Fuck you too, Dad."

One of the last things Tim recalls saying to his father, a memory nearly always securely positioned at the forefront of his thoughts.

When the hell're they gonna bust in here? Screaming whatever stupid shit they gotta say. Smack me around and leave.

Though Tim had never been in prison, let alone an alien prison, he figures the pounding footsteps and angry tones exchanged between the multitudes of voices, growing closer and easing in echo as they traverse down the hall exterior to the cell, must not be coming from an entirely peaceful species. If they are, as Tim assumes, the same excessively limbed creatures he'd encountered before, their track record supports the theory.

A door opens at the opposite end of the cell and a flood of light pours into the jailing chamber.

Tim looks around, expecting a dank dungeon with stained rings of old urine, decaying bodies, some intact, but most dismembered, blood and tissue caked on concrete and stone walls staking their hard-fast stead as the only remnants of the most unlucky of prisoners.

He sees none of this. Instead, the room is stark white and nearly completely void of feature. The musty smell of stagnating water emanates from a single drain with a five-inch diameter in the very center of the room. Tim looks to his side, expecting to see some duct paneling through which Xakdrekai might have escaped.

Nothing.

No way in or out except through the door, now standing ajar with a large boorish, greatly limbed and excessively armed creature entering the room.

Did I imagine that freak, Xakdrekai? But my arms aren't bound anymore, and I can see, for what it's worth.

The door falls shut just behind the now too familiar, ape-like, crab-legged creature. The light remains and the beast turns to face Tim with its six eyes bearing down on him with a thwarting, maniacal fixation.

Silence cascades along the four walls as Tim anticipates roaring demands and threats. Instead, somewhere in some minute depth of the still disquieting atmosphere, a sound can be heard. A movement, slight and virtually inaudible; a momentary rustling that quickly corrects itself in a hastened, panicked attempt to join the silence. With it the six-eyed head instantly cocks to the left and fixes its stare upon the wall just to the right of an unnerved Tim.

Too many moments pass as Tim fixates on the jailor with such exaggerated focus it begins to feel hypnotic with the bright and vacant background walls lending no help, only serving as canvases unto which Tim's racing and shambled thoughts paint themselves.

A great anxiety commandeers Tim's nervous and cardiovascular system. He feels as if his blood is cold and every inch of his skin is inciting itself into a riot as the flesh beneath tenses as if forming a blockade in response.

He would often exercise composure if only to support bravado, but more often than Tim would care to admit, this effort would prove futile.

Typically, an outburst of phrases like, *'fuck this'* or *'fuck you'* would find themselves commonplace in such situations involving Tim. While many may consider this a needless production of vulgarity, a sudden burst of expletives would seem to open a valve that allows the steam building within Tim to release in what is likely his least destructive manner.

Unfortunately, Tim is evidently incapable at current. In fact, the very thought of shouting anything seems hesitant to even enter into his mind.

Tim turns his attention to his right, if only to find something, anything else to draw his focus before he succumbs to a state of utter terror. He cannot immediately see whatever the other six eyes in the room are fixed upon, but in moments, a startled and gasping Xakdrekai shimmers into view through quick flashing vertical schisms of light, simply appearing in the empty space just beside Tim.

"Ach! This is not good." The alien turns to Tim and sputters out the words between hurried breaths.

"What the fuck was that?"

Tim's voice rapidly heightens to a falsetto and nearly cracks under the sudden shift in pitch.

"HIDING IN PLAIN SIGHT! What sort of fool are you? MOVE AND I WILL TERMINATE YOU BOTH!"

The mass of bellowing anger slowly steps closer to the two, now petrified, prospective escapees.

"Maybe we can *reach some sort of agreement?* I am willing to pay handsomely for this human prisoner."

"Yet, you trespass here, and attempt to release him without our consent. And any Stracbagf worth his Urellium knows NOT TO TRUST A SOESTILLIC ORGLASTICURIAN HALF-BREED."

The Stracbagf captor points its rifle directly at Xakdrekai's head and makes a vertical downward motion with the barrel indicating its wishes for Xakdrekai to kneel to the ground.

"YOU WILL ENTER INTO INDENTURED SERVITUDE UNDER THE ORDINANCE OF PRICTEX[EBR] SUB-TERRA OPERATIONS, and you do so without resistance, understood?"

Tim vaguely remembers the definition of indentured servitude as defined by his mother who often referred to her husband as a "slave-driver."

The two answer.

"Yeah, whatever." Tim.

"*Yes,* we understand." Xakdrekai.

The Stracbagf lifts Xakdrekai with one arm and twists, rotates, and flips the alien in what is likely a physical searching process. It returns Xakdrekai to the synthetic white flooring of the cell, pushing him into a sitting position as if he were little more than a doll forced into poses.

"RESTRAIN!"

The metallic cabled bindings automatically reattach to Tim's arms in an instant. Xakdrekai, too, now finds himself in similar bondage.

"How have you attained an Oral Linquistulator?" Directing the question to Xakdrekai, the stracbagf places the tip of its rifle barrel into the center of his grey-blue forehead.

"It was my father's, *second generation,* this one." Now Xakdrekai crosses his eyes attempting to stare down the rifle.

"FOOL! Those were decommissioned. They were found to generate cancerous growths in the cerebral cortex."

"In your species, yes. I am half Soestillic Orglasticurian, *on my mother's side I am*. My cells terminate in response to crowding or mutation. I can't develop cancer."

Tim simply watches as the two converse, with very little idea as to what the exchange is regarding.

"You're other half may disagree with this statement. YOU KEEP YOUR MODULATOR HALF-BREED! We shall learn how truly impervious your cell structure proves to be."

"YOU TWO WILL REMAIN IN THE DARK UNTIL WE HAVE NEED OF YOU! Let your lymph nodes be your light."

■ 5:47AM FEBRUARY 4TH 3147

By the light of the lymphatic growths on either side of Xakdrekai's head, the two prisoner's converse to pass the time until they are required for whatever labor awaits them.

"Hey..."

Tim reaches into the vast murky depths of his memory to retrieve the alien's name...and fails.

"Xakdrekai." Provides his assistance.

"Yeah, whatever. I'll just call you Xak."

"Fair enough, *my friend!*"

Tim continues.

"So hey, Xak."

"Yes, Tim."

"You suck dick."

Tim spits several beads of blood that had been collected in pustules formed within his mouth after his first encounter with the Stracbagf.

"I don't follow, *my friend!*"

"I would have just been stuck here in the dark, now I'm gonna be a fuckin' slave."

"It would have only been a matter of time, had they not decided upon *a worse fate* without my coming to rescue you."

Xakdrekai slinks in his posture and presents a clearly depressed tone.

"Shit load of good that did, Xak. Why the hell are you tryin' to rescue me anyways? You some kind of alien hero who just happens to blow chunks."

"I came to rescue you...*Because you are human!*"

The alien emphasizes after a pause as if the statement should find great significance.

"No shit, Sherlock! Big damned deal. What's it matter what I am?"

"Humans are everything. *You know?* The first divine mouth, *Krapokfles,* was very clear about your place in prophecy. I was one of the last Nabishans under his tutelage, but more and more *are converting each day!* The wisdom of Nabisha *is infinite,* and she has chosen me as her last *bah-hoo-rok-ham,* as Krapokfles successor. My first mission as a Bahuraqham was to find a human. *And I found you, my friend!*"

Tim lifts his head to stare at the ceiling and in exasperation sighs.

"What the hell? This shit just keeps piling on..."

"Why me? How'd you find me, I'm captured and thrown in jail and then you just happen to find me? What...do you live around here or something?"

"No, no, no, of course not. You'd be *hard pressed* to find anything other than Stracbagf willfully living on Edirthaimes. Most other species are '*indentured*' for these...*ra-ma-beesh* Stracbagf mining operations."

Xakdrekai spits after a short pause exaggerating his disgust with the Stracbagf.

He then lifts his clasped arms to scratch his back, but with the tight restraints, finds great difficulty in an otherwise simple task.

In response to the invasion of Xakdrekais restrained hands, a small insect native to Edirthaimes crawls away from its temporary residence, unnoticed, leaving only the three dozen eggs injected into a small section of the subcutaneous layer of fat just beneath the half-breed's skin.

"Humans are particularly difficult to find outside of the solar system, and very few non-humans dare tread there. The Stracbagf warn all to avoid it. *Quarantined is the word!* So, the only humans to be found elsewhere are likely enslaved here, *you know?*"

"Lucky me. And what's the deal with the solar system?"

Tim figures he can only humor what he now perceives to be a cultist lunatic, as this is his only current source of communication or information, no matter how zeal-addled it may be.

"Ah? *You don't know?*"

Xakdrekai sits befuddled for a moment, meaning to introduce another line of questioning, but instead respectfully answers Tim's questions before continuing with his own.

"The Stracbagf supposedly possess a weapon which can *very quickly* increase the mass of a star effectively forcing it to *become a supergiant!*"

Though nearly stupefied through the monotony of Xakdrekai's words, Tim allows him to continue filling the otherwise numbing silence with a dull monologue.

"After the third Aesthician War, they deemed humanity a threat to intergalactic harmony and sanctioned the use of all intergalactic routes through the human system with the threat that *once completing this weapon,* they will initiate first tests on Sol...Or the...What is it? *Sun!* Forcing it rapidly through supergiant growth until it explodes and becomes a super nova."

Pausing for effect, as if the previous statement should not be impactful, Xakdrekai finishes with;

"Not stopping *until your sun* becomes a black hole."

This takes Tim's attention.

But before he can offer a reply, the two are interrupted by the sudden activation of the room's light system accompanying a riotous voice booming in from somewhere overhead.

"P-I-D-S CELL ONE-THREE-EIGHT SENSORY DIMINUTION ACTIVATED. COUNTDOWN 5..."

The lights quickly grow brighter until the room appears completely white, devoid of any definition between wall, ceiling and floor. The two attempt to close their eyes but, find they are somehow incapable.

"4..."

An obnoxious, high-pitched clangor bleats repeatedly through the room and though the sound stops and the room becomes silent, the two still hear the ringing and are deaf to the remainder of the countdown, clearly not intended for the cell's occupants.

"3..."

Gaseous emissions fill the room quickly and assault the remaining senses of Tim and Xakdrekai with a combination of halothane and trace amounts of methane and sulfur dioxide quickly stripping them of consciousness.

"2..."

The gas is quickly exhausted from the room through a sophisticated ventilation system as the lights are dimmed until returning to their previous activated state.

"1..."

Timmothy and Xakdrekai lie motionless, lightly propped against the back of the cell as their shackles gently release and retract into the walls.

"P-I-D-S CELL ONE-THREE-EIGHT PRIMED FOR EVACUATION."

*What will happen to **Tim** and **Xakdrekai**?*

*Will the **Chapel brothers** ever **reunite**?*

*Whatever happened to **Pete**?*

Who cares?

**THESE QUESTIONS AND MORE
WILL BE ANSWERED IN:**

BOOK

(RELUCTANT) TRIPS **2**

WITHOUT **REASONABLE
CONVEYANCE**
(OR) FROM HERE TO THERE

COMING SOMETIME!
(PROBABLY)